S0-BFB-867

A GRAVE SITUATION

A GRAVE
SITUATION

•

ELLEN GRAY MASSEY

AVALON BOOKS
THOMAS BOUREGY AND COMPANY, INC.
401 LAFAYETTE STREET
NEW YORK, NEW YORK 10003

FIc
MAS
R

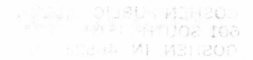

PRINTED IN THE UNITED STATES OF AMERICA
ON ACID-FREE PAPER
BY HADDON CRAFTSMEN, SCRANTON, PENNSYLVANIA

To my sister, Miriam Gray,
who grew up in the early 1900's
hearing the story of the unknown grave,
and after her retirement back to the family home,
tried unsuccessfully to find some hard facts about it.

Author's Note

Five miles west of Nevada, Missouri, beside the tracks of the old Katy Railroad, there actually is an unknown grave just as I've described it. The site, the legends surrounding it, and the railroad men tending to the grave for almost a hundred and twenty years are all true, as is the *Unsolved Mysteries* segment about it on television. However, the Greenlee and Lewis families, and their solution to the mystery of the murdered woman buried there, are entirely fictitious. Intrigued with this unknown grave which is only two miles from my family farm, I've tried for years to come up with a plausible explanation for it. This is my solution. Like young Lexie Greenlee in my story, I turned my imagination loose.

E.G.M.

Chapter One

T he pointer scratched the leg of Pippa's jeans with his front paw for attention. Mechanically she stroked his head and fondled his velvet ears while he pressed his tall, lean body against her, trembling as pointers do. The long shadows from the late-afternoon sun carpeted the lawn and the slice of the barnyard she could see from the patio. She paused for the first time during this long day's work on the farm—a day of harvesting the last of the soybeans on the west field, delivering the final truckload to the elevator in town, putting up the combine for the year, and finishing the evening feeding.

The sunlight flickered in the water trough she had just filled. Crickets were beginning to sing from the woodsy lot behind the barn, adding their voices to the persistent drone of hundreds of katydids high in the trees. There was a whirl and flutter of wings, followed by the subdued chatter of a flock of migrating birds landing in the orange-red maple tree by the fence. Yet the farm was quiet and peaceful. Pippa ignored the

3

hum of a slow vehicle on the road, just as she had long ago learned to shut out the roar of the locomotives on the Katy Railroad track across the country road from her house.

She sat on the edge of the concrete patio, trying hard to swallow the sighs that surfaced whenever she slowed down long enough to remember. In contrast to her mood, his tail wagging happily, the dog rested his chin on her lap, his unblinking eyes pleading for her attention. The yellow tabby cat, purring loudly as he stalked back and forth, rubbed his arched back against her side and pushed his nose under her arm to make her stroke him. A cacophony of squeals from the barnyard helped lighten her mood more than either the dog or cat had done. The commotion announced the arrival of the Angora goat, who butted her way through the hogs. Then flattening her whole body lengthwise against the woven wire fence separating them, the goat positioned herself as close to the house as possible.

Pippa sighed, catching a sob in her throat before it surfaced. She cupped the dog's head in both hands and shook it lovingly. "Oh, Rainy, thanks for your company, big boy, but I can't stop missing him."

Then she reached over to pick up the cat to try to hold him in her arms, but he struggled out of her grasp. "Sorry, Freewill," she said, putting him down. "I know you don't like to be held, but I need to hug something." Instead she hugged Rainy. The spotted dog trembled with delight.

Satisfied with her day's achievements, and relaxing in the crisp coolness for a few minutes before she had to drive to her parents to pick up the boys, she didn't hold back memories of Doug.

On beautiful evenings such as this after the twins were in bed and he and she had cleaned up after a long day's work on the farm, they used to sit here silently admiring their world, content with the present and full of plans. Usually she was the one who came out first, and missing her, he would appear from behind to put both arms around her. They wouldn't say much, but would just soak in the stillness, contentment, and fulfillment of their love. After a bit, they would go in.

As she sat there alone she could still feel his muscular arms as he used to hug her. She could still sense the freshness of his body straight from the shower. Everything in sight radiated his presence. The lilac bush he reset and was so fond of, the fences he built, the hand gate, and the big metal machinery barn—all glowed in the horizontal sun rays. Bathed in the magic highlights, her farm—her present reality—seemed as illusive as the past two years had been. Surely those years that were a dream from which she would awaken and then tell him her every sensation, just as they always used to do.

Another sigh escaped her. She tightened her grip on the pointer. Rainy wiggled in pleasure. The past two years, and today, were real—as solid as the cool concrete she was sitting on. And as obvious as the dust hanging in the air from the car crawling up the road. It was those ten previous years that now seemed unreal, in spite of the substantial evidence all about her to prove their existence.

An annoyed moo diverted her attention to the barnyard. Possessively, the goat butted back some calves that came to the water tank near the gate to get a drink.

"Rube, stop that!" Pippa ordered. Admonished, the goat returned to her stance against the fence.

The calves had done well. Doug would be proud of how well she and the boys had raised them. The Angus herd out in the pasture and the hogs had increased too. She'd kept everything going. She could see his pride in her shining from those blue eyes that smiled at her so often.

A deep sob overwhelmed her before she could swallow it. Pushing Rainy away, she laid her head on her arms and wept. She was never one to cry before. Lately, as now, when alone she sometimes broke down without warning.

Rainy, Doug's hunting partner, had completely transferred his affections. He now looked at her with his worried brown eyes, wondering what this was all about. The big tom, the only one of the dozen cats they owned that Doug claimed as his, continued to purr and rub against her arm and back. Still pressed against the fence, Rube was ready to follow her anywhere, even into the house if she could get through the fence. Doug's saddle mare lifted her head from her feed box and nickered to her. She was their world now—he a distant or forgotten memory.

Even the boys seemed content now; they rarely spoke of their father anymore. Their loss was only half a loss. They still had her. Their lives were not disrupted.

And the farmland? Fertile but passive, capable of creating and nourishing life, but responding only when acted upon. And it continued to produce, unmindful of who worked it.

Everything depended on her. The once-shared pleasures had become lonely obligations. She was alone in

the twilight of another of a long line of endless days, with everything she loved around her except the one person who made it all worthwhile.

The wind blew cooler and stronger. The unlatched wooden gate to the barnyard bumping gently against the post gave a rhythmic bass to the shrill katydids. A lone whippoorwill from the woodlot added its monotonous harmony. A vehicle—she unconsciously recognized it as the same expensive-looking, dusty van that passed twice before—crept back down the road.

How can I keep on going? she thought despairingly.

The beauty of the mid-October day intensified her aloneness because Doug's presence was all around. His fine new combine and tractor with enclosed cab, the animals he raised, the land which had been in his family for generations that he improved and farmed—he was everywhere, just as his spirit was always with her, sharing in every act and thought.

As usual when she allowed herself to release her grief, she felt better. He seemed to be sitting beside her, reminding her that she would find happiness again. She would do all right. She had taken care of everything, their sons, the animals, and the land. "Why, even today," she imagined him saying, "you've finished combining the soybeans. All that's left is to plant that field in wheat. A piece of cake!"

She smiled through her tears. Yes, of course she would continue. Was there any other choice? She lifted her head. He was still helping her. Without this belief she would have given up months ago.

She gave Rainy a final hug, petted Freewill, and started toward the pickup to drive the few miles to her parents' home to pick up her boys. Rainy, his lean body wiggling in anticipation of a ride, jumped into the back of the truck, his head peering around the cab as if already riding down the road.

"Whoa there! Get back!" A deep voice penetrated her thoughts, drawing her attention to the far side of the road where a business-style van was pulled over as far as possible without getting into the ditch.

"Hey, lady, this your goat?" A medium-size young man was sprinting back across the road to his van. Rube, her white curly head lowered and ready to charge if he made one step closer to the house, had him effectively barricaded.

Wiping away the last tears, Pippa remembered the gate swinging in the breeze. As usual, sneaky Rube had found an exit out of the barnyard.

Pippa ran to the middle of the road and grabbed one of Rube's horns. "Yeah, she's my goat. She won't hurt you."

"She looks like she means business to me," the man said, cautiously eyeing the goat from behind the open driver's door of his van. He removed his wide-brimmed hat and wiped his forehead with his sleeve before replacing it.

Rube struggled to reach the man, her little front hooves showering gravel behind her and her head lowered menacingly, ready to butt. To control the goat, Pippa straddled the animal's back, grasping a curved-back horn with each hand. The twins often rode Rube in this manner.

"I'm sorry. I guess I left the gate unlatched. Rube is very protective. She especially doesn't like men with beards."

The man stroked his neatly trimmed, auburn beard.

His eyes, though still wary of the goat, were beginning to smile as they sized up the work-stained woman in front of him.

"Maybe you'd like to put the goat back in her pen?" he suggested in a light tone. He was sitting in the driver's seat ready to shut the open door if the goat pulled out of Pippa's control.

She laughed. "Yeah. Good idea." She pulled Rube's head around to leave and then turned to ask, "I noticed you've been cruising up and down the road. Are you lost?"

"I'm not sure. I saw you out back of your house and thought I'd ask before it gets too dark to see."

"Sure, where're you headed?" Remembering her manners, she introduced herself. While keeping a firm grip on one of Rube's horns with her left hand, she extended her right one.

Though he was looking at her eyes, he was taking in everything—her short, boyish-cut hair, which was the exact color of her eyes and persisted in falling into her face, her tall slim figure dressed in dirt- and oil-stained work clothes, even her tear-smeared face.

"I'm Pippa Greenlee," she said, wondering if he had noticed her crying back on the patio. His hand was firm and hard. She noticed some bright-colored stains on it.

As if her name was good news, his face lit up. "Then I'm not lost," he said, relieved. "I've been driving all over this end of the county. A man in town headed me in this direction and told me you could help me. I'm Cotter Lewis from Texas."

"You're a long way from home. How can I help

you?'' She grinned as she added, ''You obviously didn't come here to buy any of my goats!''

''Hardly.'' Still holding the door between him and the goat, he added, ''But I can wait until you put that goat behind a stout fence.''

Smiling, Pippa ran with Rube to the barnyard gate, pushed the unwilling goat inside with her knee, and latched the gate securely this time. ''Now, girl, stay put. You can't go butting people out on the road. They have a right to be there.'' Though her voice was stern, she ruined the disciplinary effect by shaking her head indulgently and patting Rube on her head.

Realizing that he wouldn't be getting a ride after all, Rainy leaped out of the pickup and ran over to the stranger, tail wagging and tongue hanging out of his panting mouth. When Pippa returned, the pointer was luxuriating in the stranger's caresses.

''At least your dog is friendly,'' the Texan said.

''He's sure no watchdog. Rube takes care of that department well enough for all of us.'' She pushed back the strand of hair that fell over her right eye.

''Good dog,'' he said, studying Rainy's conformation. ''How's he on quail?''

''Fine. Only he hasn't been hunted for a couple of years.''

Cotter's forehead wrinkled and he pushed up the brim of his brown hat as if surprised that someone who didn't hunt would keep such a good hunting dog.

''Now how can I help you?'' Pippa asked.

''I heard there is someone buried here on this stretch of the railroad right-of-way—some legend about an unknown grave that's been tended by the railroad workers for over a hundred years.''

Pippa nodded her head. "That's right."

Encouraged by her agreement, he continued, "But I've driven up and down this whole mile and can't find it. I was going to walk the track, but didn't think I'd have time this afternoon. Know anything about it?"

"Yeah. You've parked your van right by it."

Pippa crossed the road, climbed the rickety barbed-wire fence running between the tracks and the road, and parted back the waist-high weeds to reveal a well-cared-for grave site about ten feet from the tracks.

Cotter stroked his beard in amazement. Then he walked slowly around the cleared space, unmindful of the chiggers and the stick-me-tights, tramping down the circling weeds with his decorated boots.

"Can you beat that? It's really here!" he said in disbelief.

"Sure, it's here. Isn't that what you expected?"

"Well, yes. It's what I heard, but the whole story seems too bizarre to be real."

He squatted on his haunches and studied the grave. Neatly placed and smoothed-out white gravel covered a mound of about four by six feet, bordered all around with small round sandstone rocks. At the west end was a wind-worn, upright, and unmarked rough sandstone slab and another smaller one lying flat at the foot. A cluster of faded and bent pink plastic tulips were by the headstone where they had been stuck into the ground.

"Remarkable," Cotter said, vaulting back over the fence to get his camera case from his van.

"Every year around Memorial Day somebody comes by and cleans off the grave, rakes the gravel back around it, and leaves some flowers or a wreath," Pippa said.

"And they have been doing that for years?"

"Since about 1870-something, so the story goes. For the last twelve years—that's since I've lived here—it's been like you see it."

"Incredible!" Cotter was busy taking photographs, jotting down notes, and switching lenses.

Pippa was surprised at the Texan's reaction. Ever since she could remember, she'd known of this grave and the legend surrounding it. Everyone in the county did. No big deal. It was something she'd always known and didn't seem incredible. Then when she married and moved to the Greenlee place, since it was literally at her door, the grave became part of her everyday living like the railroad or the big maple trees. Sometimes she noticed railroad section men repairing the tracks or replacing worn ties, but she never saw them actually working on the grave site—all she saw was evidence that they had. Come to think of it, it was sort of eerie. And incredible.

From the number of shots Cotter took and his ease with his equipment, Pippa guessed he must be a professional photographer. He was probably here to write a feature. The last story written about the grave that she knew about was in 1988 by a reporter from the *Kansas City Star*. It seemed that every so often someone got the urge to dredge up the story. Not surprising; after all, everyone is intrigued by an unsolved mystery. Pippa herself was interested when she first moved here, collecting all she could find out about it.

Since she'd lived on the Greenlee farm, a few curious

people had come to her house looking for the grave. Even some television people. But they got it all wrong.

While Cotter was studying the site, Pippa started to leave. The sun, already hid by the Osage orange hedgerow bordering her neighbor's field across the tracks, was splashing red-orange color over the few scattered clouds. It would soon be dark. She had to get the boys. If she didn't put them to bed soon, she'd have trouble getting them up for school tomorrow. Besides, they had probably worn her parents to a frazzle by now.

Followed closely by Rainy, once again excited about a ride, she climbed back through the fence to cross the road.

"I have to go now," she said in parting. Still squatting beside the unmarked headstone as she left, Cotter waved his thanks.

Just as Pippa drove her pickup into the road, with Rainy's panting mouth near her open window where he was peering around the cab, Cotter waved his hat for her to stop. "Thanks for showing me the grave. Could I come back sometime? I want to find out all you know about it."

"Sure. I'm here most of the time, though you may have to hunt for me out in the fields. I've got to get my boys now. They're at my parents' place down the highway." She pointed generally south and drove off, hiding Cotter and his van in a cloud of gray dust.

As she drove the few miles to her parents' house, she realized she wasn't tired anymore and her spasm of grief hadn't left her depressed as it usually did. In fact, she hardly thought about herself as she was reviewing in her mind what she did know about the unknown grave. The Texan's enthusiasm was infectious.

The way old-timers told the story was that about 1876 at Ellis, a young woman and a man got off the eastbound Katy Flyer of the Missouri Kansas and Texas Railroad. At that time there was a depot and some siding tracts at the little village not quite a mile west of the Greenlee farm. Since nobody knew the couple, and it was unusual for anyone but local people to use that stop, the people at the station were curious about them and remembered their actions.

The young woman was pretty and fashionably dressed. She carried only a small handbag. Her companion was a young man, also fashionably dressed. No one remembered his having any luggage.

The woman seemed distraught, and jumped off the passenger car first, followed by the man just before the train pulled out. They were arguing, though no one remembered hearing anything they said. Since Ellis was a whistle-stop, the train paused only long enough to discharge the passengers. The couple argued beside the train until it left. Then the woman started walking rapidly east down the tracks. The man ran to catch up. As far as the onlookers at Ellis could see them until they disappeared into the twilight and the vegetation along the road that paralleled the tracks, the two people were still arguing, the woman slightly ahead of the man, who was gesturing wildly.

This action in itself was strange behavior. Those at Ellis talked about it for a few minutes, wondering who the couple was, but assumed they were on their way to visit relatives at some nearby farm. As the people dispersed to their various activities, they forgot about the couple.

About two days later in the lush prairie grass beside the tracks, a farmer hunting some stray hogs found the body of the young woman. There were gunshot wounds in her chest, but no marks on her clothing or handbag that gave a clue as to her identity. The inquest and search for her companion were equally unproductive. No one ever learned the woman's identity, why she was murdered, or who her companion was. The man had vanished.

Katy Railroad section hands buried the body where it was found. For these many years workers from the railroad had tended the grave.

As Pippa thought over these mysterious happenings, she understood why the stranger from Texas was excited. Someone somewhere must have known something. The woman couldn't just have dropped out of nowhere. And the man? Surely he must have confided in someone. But after a hundred and twenty years. . . .

Pulling into her parents' driveway, she put these thoughts out of her mind as she spied her two sons watching for her out the window. Before she could stop the truck, they erupted from the house, carrying school backpacks and jackets. Behind them her parents appeared in the door, waving and smiling. Her father had his arm around her mother's waist. How lucky they were to reach old age together!

Over Rainy's excited barking, each boy tried to outshout the other, telling her about Grandma's cookies, the door they helped Grandpa fix, and their day at school.

"I finished the soybeans," Pippa managed to tell

her father over the hubbub. He gave her a thumbs-up sign.

She did not feel the pain of the empty place in her heart.

Chapter Two

"Did you have any trouble finishing the soy-beans?" one of the twins asked, his freckled face serious now that he had exhausted the fund of his day's activities.

"Not a bit, Vance. I finished before noon. Then I took the last load to the elevator, and I even put up the combine. All done."

"Good." Vance leaned back against the seat, sitting even closer to his mother in contrast to his brother by the window who was sitting on the edge of the seat, not missing a thing on the road.

"Got the check yet?" Vance asked.

"No, sweetie." Pippa patted his knee. "I'll go settle up tomorrow. The beans did well, forty bushels to the acre. We did okay."

Realizing how tired she was, she moved her shoulders back and forth to relax them. Vance's tone caused her to glance briefly from the road to look at him. His face was still puckered in thought.

"Why'd you ask? You remember this morning I told you that I wouldn't come for you until I finished."

Vance nodded.

"You shouldn't worry so much."

"Well, Lexie and I figured that you'd finish early, but when you didn't come until we'd had supper, I thought something must have happened."

"No, I came right away." Perhaps the boys were big enough not to be shunted off to their grandparents when there was important work to do. Next time she'd let them be with her—especially Vance.

She slowed down to make the right turn onto the gravel road to her place. In the fading light she noticed the Texan's van pulled off the highway at the intersection, almost into the weeds on the edge of the triangular road right-of-way.

"Oh, I almost forgot. I guess I *was* a bit late. I had a visitor." She pointed to the van.

Both boys craned to see. "Who? I don't see anybody," Lexie said.

"I never saw that van before," Vance said, his forehead puckering again. "What's it doing parked there?"

Pippa wasn't paying attention to the boys' questions as she made the turn and, barely moving, looked closely at the van. The back doors were wide open. Inside the dome light showed the rudiments of living quarters with boxes, packages, boards, easels, and photographic equipment stashed in every conceivable spot. The Texan was not in sight.

"That was my visitor," she said as she inched down the gravel road.

"Who?" Lexie asked, his blond head sticking out the window. He repeated, "I don't see anybody."

"The man must be around somewhere. Oh, there he is." She spotted him on the far side of the van. He turned toward them and waved.

"Who's he?" Vance asked.

"Someone from Texas. He stopped on the road in front of our house just as I was ready to come after you guys. Rube had him treed in his van." She smiled, remembering how quickly Cotter retreated from the goat. She told the boys how he looked and what he was doing at their place.

Lexie laughed. "I wish I'd seen it."

"Good for ol' Rube," Vance agreed. Just as they turned into their drive, once again serious, he said, "Mom, Lexie and I ought to be here with you after school. We're almost ten now. We can help you."

Lexie agreed.

"And protect me from strangers from Texas?" she added, knowing that was what Vance was thinking.

Vance grinned self-consciously.

"And so you won't miss out on all the action?" she teased Lexie.

Lexie screwed up his face into a look that said, "You can't put anything over on Mom."

"You're right, guys. You *are* old enough and I need you."

The grinning boys made a high-five sign. "From now on come straight home from school," she said, "and change into your work clothes. If I'm not in the house, I'll leave you a note where to find me on the farm. We'll do the work together."

"Aw-right!" Vance shouted.

"Cool!" Lexie said, his tanned face beaming in pride.

"Partners?" she asked.

"Yeah," they both said.

Lexie tumbled out of the pickup, and, followed by Rainy, dashed into the house. Throwing on all the lights, including the yard light, he left the kitchen door open, dropped his school pack on the table, upsetting the sugar bowl, and tossed his jacket in the general direction of a chair.

Vance, however, piled his belongings neatly on the edge of the patio before running to the fence to pet Rube, who, as usual, was at the lawn gate the minute she heard the pickup pulling into the drive.

"Good ol' Rube," Vance said, squatting beside her and throwing both arms around her neck. Rube rubbed her head up and down the boy's side. Grabbing her horns, he swung his leg over her woolly back. Dutifully, the goat trotted around the barnyard. His feet tucked under her belly so they wouldn't drag on the ground, Vance yelled and waved one hand in the air as if riding a bronco at a rodeo. Rainy raced after them, barking his delight. The pigs and calves scattered in all directions. Joining in the fun, the mare galloped around her paddock and came full speed toward the fence that separated her from the goat and rider and slid to a stop just before reaching it.

Only the cat was unaffected. Perched on the doorstep where the patio light reflected off his yellow coat, he calmly washed his face, patiently waiting for someone less rambunctious than Lexie to open the door for him.

Pippa groaned. So much for the twins becoming the men of the family. It'd be a long time before they could replace. . . .

The pain that resurfaced choked the reprimands she

had ready. She didn't scold Lexie for being careless with his things or Vance for dirtying his good school clothes. Instead, she watched Vance for a moment, and let her eyes roam over the part of her farm illuminated by the light pole. "They'll improve with time," she said out loud to the farm in general. "But will I?"

She refused to let the inner makings of a sob climb up her throat. Not in front of the boys. Besides, there was too much to do. Her stomach growled, reminding her she hadn't eaten. She opened the kitchen door and stepped in after Freewill scampered ahead of her. Lexie was ineffectively brushing the sugar off the table. Scattered over the table was an opened loaf of bread, lettuce and tomatoes, and an empty package of lunch meat. A sloppy but thick sandwich rested on a plate ready for her meal.

Vance stomped in. "Hey, Mom! Did you finish all the feeding?"

"Yes. Did you latch the gate?"

"Of course. Rube promised me she wouldn't get out."

"That'll be the day." Lexie laughed.

There was hope yet; the boys were maturing. Pippa grinned at her helpers and gratefully drank the milk Lexie poured for her. She relished his juicy sandwich, even though mayonnaise oozed out and ran down her fingers as she took each bite. The boys helped her finish what was left of Grandma's apple cobbler.

Glad that the day was over, that the last crop of the year was harvested, that the boys were growing—there were many good things to be pleased about—she pushed back from the table. Freewill was curled up in the hollow of the pillow in the rocking chair, purring softly from Lexie's caresses. The Greenlee heirloom clock ticked its never-ending rhythmic order to the room. The furnace kicked on, dispelling the October chill. Pippa yawned. Although it was time the boys were in bed, she really didn't want them to leave. Their chatter and vitality kept at bay the sad memories of the ends of other successful days when Doug and she would relax here in comfort and. . . .

Vance first noticed the commotion in the barnyard— a muted thud followed by a metallic clank. They all recognized the familiar noise of Rube butting her head against the gate to get out of the lot. Only this time the rapid and angry thuds were disturbing the other animals. The pigs grunted and squealed; the calves lowed.

"I better go see." Pippa sighed. There was no end to the demands on her. This animal was getting to be more trouble than she was worth. "You guys get ready for bed."

Instead of obeying her, they both followed her out the kitchen door. All three of them were momentarily frightened as they collided into someone on the patio.

"Are you sure that gate will hold her?" asked a man's voice.

Recognizing her earlier visitor, Pippa let out her breath in relief. "Not if she's determined to get out. Vance, go put her in the shed before she breaks down the gate." When the boy didn't move, she added, "This is the man I told you about that was interested in the unknown grave."

"Oh," Vance said, still without moving. Rube's lunges at the gate were more frantic.

"These are my sons, Vance and Lexie," Pippa said. "Mr.—Oh, I've forgotten your name."

"Lewis, Cotter Lewis. Just call me Cotter."

The Texan impressed both boys by shaking hands with each of them as if they were grown men. "Think you can corral that wild animal before she knocks me over, Vance?" he asked.

"Sure." Vance ran to the gate.

"She doesn't like strangers," Lexie said, trying to size up Cotter.

"So I've learned."

" 'Specially strangers with beards," he added, fascinated with the man's neatly trimmed beard and mustache that framed his mouth, but didn't extend under his chin nor to his sideburns.

"I never saw anyone with a beard like that," Lexie said, staring at Cotter's face.

"It's a goatee," Pippa said quietly to hush him up. His rudeness embarrassed her.

"No wonder Rube doesn't like him. His beard is better'n hers." Lexie laughed at his own wit.

Meanwhile, Vance struggled with the unwilling goat. "Maybe Lexie is right," Cotter said, stroking his beard. "Animals usually like me." Rainy was leaning against his leg like an old friend, begging to be noticed. Cotter scratched him behind his ears.

"I'm sorry to bother you again, Mrs. Greenlee, but when I saw you come back, I thought now might be a good time to ask you some questions about the unknown grave. Tomorrow you'll probably be busy."

With Rube safely locked in the shed, and all of them seated in the living room, Pippa started the story of the unknown woman buried by the tracks.

"And that's why we have a ghost here," Lexie blurted out, interrupting her.

"Stupid, there's no ghost," Vance said, disgusted.

Pippa laughed at Lexie. "He's got quite an imagination," she said to Cotter.

"She's stuck here until someone finds out who she is," Lexie said and sat straight with his lips pressed tight together.

"More of your dumb detective stories," Vance said.

"Guys, that's enough. Lexie, no more interruptions." She turned to Cotter. "Lexie loves to solve mysteries." She then told him everything she'd heard about the unknown grave. As she progressed in the story, Cotter's interest deepened. He alternately stroked his beard and clenched and unclenched his hands in his excitement.

"It all fits," he said, slamming his right fist into his left palm. Then he explained what he meant and why he was so interested in the grave. He also had a story to tell. Just as Pippa had grown up hearing the legend of the unknown grave, Cotter had grown up with the story of a several-times-over great-aunt who disappeared. He told them his story.

Back in Denison, Texas, in the spring of 1876, his ancestor's eighteen-year-old daughter, Ivy Lewis, fell in love with a man from another state, a man nobody in her family knew anything about. Though he had no job, he had plenty of money—dressed in expensive clothes and drove fine horses—but was silent about his background. Ivy's family couldn't understand how she could be attracted to him because to them he was effeminate, surly, and argumentative. No one else liked him.

The courtship lasted for a few months, Ivy being more taken with him as time went by. Cotter surmised that her attachment to him might have been as much rebellion as attraction because the family was so opposed to it. The father eventually forbade her to see him and made plans to send her to distant relatives in order to separate them.

However, sometime in the night before Ivy was to leave, she ran away. After that night neither she nor the man was ever seen or heard from again, though the family and authorities searched diligently for several months. They had only two clues: witnesses saw the couple at the train station waiting for the westbound late-night sleeper, and her mother found a brief note pinned to her pillow the next morning.

The note, dated the previous night, read:

> *Don't try to find me, for Herb and I will be far away from here when you read this. You'll never see me again. I won't let you separate us. I love him and will follow him wherever he goes.*

Cotter said, "The note is still in the old family Bible, though the ink is faded and the paper yellow by now."

"Did anyone ever hear from them again?" Lexie asked. Though Vance was almost asleep, Lexie hung on every word.

"Nothing. Not a single lead. It was as if they were swallowed up by the earth. Ivy's story has been told generation after generation at family gatherings. I remember as kids, my cousins and I tried to figure out what could have happened. We made up all kinds of outlandish stories. We'd try to outdo one another. I remember one I especially liked was that they went to California, hijacked a ship, and became pirates.''

"Maybe they were picked up by a UFO and taken to another planet," Lexie said, making motor noises and using his hands to picture a spaceship landing and taking off.

"Now that's a possibility we didn't think of," Cotter said, as he and Pippa laughed.

"Well, maybe that's what happened." Lexie's feelings were hurt that everyone was laughing at him. "It's as good as them being pirates.''

Cotter wiped the grin off his face and forced himself to speak seriously. "You're right, Lexie. No one knows.''

"Then you think," Pippa asked, "that our unknown grave may be hers?''

"It's a possibility." He looked at Lexie. "A better one than becoming pirates, don't you think?''

Lexie twisted his mouth in thought. "But you said they took the train *west*. This is *east* of Texas.''

"Yes, west is what everyone thought. All the investigation was to the west, but no one actually *saw* them get on that train. Maybe they just wanted people to *think* they went west but came east instead. Or to throw them off, got on the west train and then down the line somewhere switched to one coming east." He waved his arm in the direction of the road and railroad track. "Your railroad out there, it also went through her town, less than a day's ride away.''

Vance asked, "How'd you find out about this grave now after all this time?''

"That's an amazing coincidence. Early last summer

I was working hard in my studio all day getting ready for the summer and fall art fair circuit. To keep awake, I turned on the television. I didn't care what I saw. The show was a rerun of *Unsolved Mysteries*. Ever see that program?''

"Yeah," both boys said.

"Lexie likes to try to invent solutions," Pippa said.

"And he gets mad when the mysteries are later solved and it wasn't anything like what he imagined," Vance teased.

Lexie poked Vance, who pushed him back.

"Well, that was the first time I'd seen it," Cotter said. "So I think that it was quite remarkable that on that particular segment one of the unsolved mysteries was about an unknown grave in western Missouri."

"That was our grave," Vance said. "The TV guys were here. They started to tramp all over our yard until Rube ran them off."

"We saw the show, and taped it too," Lexie said.

"But they got the facts all screwed up," Pippa said. "They tried to make it fit some missing woman from Iowa or someplace up north. The woman they featured disappeared in 1910 and the family thought that a possible solution to her disappearance might be this unknown grave. If the TV people had done any research, asked anyone, even my boys here, they would have learned that our woman was buried much earlier than that."

"Yeah," Cotter said. "That's what I discovered. Even at the end of that segment on the show, the announcer admitted that some local people believed that this grave was as early as the late 1800s. I wasn't paying too much attention, but when he said that, I got to thinking that this might be my ancestor buried here.''

Though only mildly attentive before, Vance became interested. "You mean you know who the woman was?''

"Well, no. Only a hunch. You see, I'm into genealogy, so after the TV show, I jotted down some notes and filed them away to do some digging into it later when I wasn't so busy. You see, my season was just starting.''

When their questioning looks told him they didn't understand, he explained. "I'm an artist and photographer. Each summer and fall I make a tour of certain arts and crafts festivals to show and sell my work. I've just now been to my last one this season down in north Arkansas. During the rest of the year, I prepare my work for the next season.'' Freewill jumped up into his lap. Cotter stroked him under his chin.

"And you live in your van?'' Vance asked. "We saw it up at the corner.''

"While on tour, yes.''

"Cool,'' Lexie said, his eyes shining.

"When I finished packing up after the Arkansas show and looked at the map, I realized that I was less than a hundred miles from this grave site. I didn't have my notes with me, and all I could remember about the location was that it was in this county. So I drove to your courthouse this morning. I spent most of the day trying to find someone who could tell me where the grave was. I began to think that even the location of the grave was as unknown as its occupant. I finally contacted a man in the county historical society who told me it was near the Greenlee farm.''

While Cotter was talking, Pippa was matching the similarities of his story and hers. Just as the Texan had often tried to imagine what happened to his predecessor, she had frequently invented solutions to the woman in the unknown grave. Only she could never think of any possibility to fit the known facts.

Cotter had a missing woman; she had the grave of an unknown woman. Was it possible that the two women were the same?

"Let's analyze the two stories," Pippa said, thoroughly intrigued with the mystery.

"It's the same railroad," Lexie blurted before either of the adults could speak.

"Right," Cotter said. "If I'm not mistaken, and I'll check on that, the Katy Flyer that came through Denison in Texas came right past here."

"I'll write this down," Lexie said, his brown eyes dancing with pleasure at being included in the conversation. He was taken with this stranger who from the first introduction kept the twins' names straight. Maybe his mother would forget about their bedtime. Mysteries were his bag. He scrambled in his notebook for a clean sheet of paper and scribbled down the first clue, *Katy Flyer in both places*.

"If she got on the Flyer in Denison sometime late that night or early the next morning, the timing for her to get to Ellis in the late afternoon is about right," Cotter said.

"The date is about the same—1876," Pippa said.

"What month was the woman here buried?" Cotter asked.

"I don't know. Some accounts even have the date more like the 1890s, but most agree on 1876. About twenty years ago, a member of the historical society wrote the railroad to find out the exact date, but they didn't have any records that far back. Maybe we could search through the newspaper morgue, or the sheriff's old files. There was an inquest. But I doubt if there's any record. Things were still pretty unsettled around here after the Civil War.''

"The letter Ivy left was dated May 14," Cotter said.

Lexie was getting restless. "What should I put down?"

"Just write down both in 1876," Pippa said.

"Both women were the same age," Vance said.

"Ivy was eighteen. What about the dead woman?" Cotter asked.

"Nothing, except she was young."

"Close enough," Cotter said. "Put that down, Lexie. And the woman was fashionably dressed, you said. My relatives were well-to-do for that time. I'm sure she would have been well dressed."

"There was a man in both cases," Pippa said.

"Yeah."

"They were arguing," Lexie said. "Maybe that means that Ivy's parents were right and she found out what a dweeb he really was and she wanted out."

"Good point," Cotter said. Then he turned to Pippa. "You've got some smart boys here."

Pippa looked fondly from one to the other. "Yes, I have. They will be ten next month and just tonight we have become partners." Her fond look turned stern when from the kitchen she heard the clock striking off another hour. "Now young men, that does not mean you can stay up all night on a school night. To bed with you."

Both boys objected, loudly pleading. Lexie was almost crying with disappointment. Here he was on a hot trail to solving his first real mystery. And poof! Just like that he had to go bed like a baby.

"I know the solution to this problem," Cotter said as he stood up, carefully removing Freewill from his lap and putting him on the floor. "I should leave. Your mother's right, boys. It *is* late, not only for you but for your mother and me."

Defeated, the boys murmured their good nights.

"Lexie," Cotter said, "may I have your list? You've all been a great help. Maybe we can all solve another mystery sometime."

Lexie handed him the list, shaking his head as if Cotter were completely stupid. "This one's not solved yet."

Chapter Three

The next afternoon Pippa watched for the school
bus. The field she was disking bordered the state highway, so that she could spot the bus before it turned
down the county road to her house.

Since she had worked all afternoon with no break-
downs, she didn't want to stop while the work was
going so well. Comfortably seated in the glassed-in
cabin of the big John Deere tractor, she was pleased
with herself. In town this morning when she settled up
the soybean crop, she was able to pay all the bills,
including the semiannual note on the combine, and put
the rest in her account. She had worked on her budget
so much that she knew the figures by heart. If the price
of yearling steers held a few more weeks until the grass
was gone and she could sell them, and with the sale
of the shoats in about a month, she would be in good
shape until next spring.

For the first time since Doug's death, she could
measure real progress. She had already paid off the big
tractor. Just four more payments on the combine and

she'd be out of debt—at least for a while. By then she'd probably need to replace some piece of equipment.

Thank goodness the farm was clear. It was long held in the Greenlee family, and Pippa was determined that she would keep it for her sons. She figured she could run it for ten more years, maybe less, and then turn it over to the boys. Probably Vance would be the one to stay, she guessed.

With the disking going so smoothly, preparing the ground for wheat, she almost regretted her decision for the boys to come home rather than go to their grandparents'. She must watch for them to come home, stop work, and then have them underfoot. Her parents' standing offer to keep the kids whenever she needed a baby-sitter had been a godsend, allowing her to work longer, uninterrupted hours. Why not continue that arrangement? The boys were still children. In a couple more years they would be big enough to really help rather than be a hindrance. Had she made the right decision?

The emptiness inside her ached. If Doug hadn't died, the boys would be helping out regularly by now. Even before, he had them doing easy jobs, learning the operations of their big stock and grain farm. One or the other was always with him, the other trailing after her. When the complete load landed on her shoulders alone, and she couldn't handle everything—her grief, running the sixteen-hundred-acre farm, and the young sons—she relied on her parents to watch the boys. She had shunted them off.

Well, no more. She would come in from the fieldwork for the day when they got home. Together they would do chores around the house and barn.

As she watched the dried bean stalks being cut to pieces and ground into the smoothed-out black soil behind her, she wondered again if she'd made a wise decision. Ahead of her was a whole section of field that she could prepare in just a couple more hours. Maybe she could even finish the field if she worked an hour or so under the tractor lights.

She glanced uneasily at the sky. Still clear. Tomorrow promised to be another good day, but the weather was unpredictable. Tomorrow might bring a rainy spell that could last several days. Every day made a difference this late in the season. She figured a half day tomorrow to finish the disking, and another day to plant.

But weren't the boys more important than a wheat crop? What would Doug say? She didn't have to guess; she knew. Family always came first with him. One could gamble that the crops would do well, that the weather would be favorable, and that the price of hogs would improve in the spring—most farming is a gamble—but one should never gamble with the lives of family members. There would always be another year to grow wheat. The year the twins turned ten would never come again.

The rest of the field could wait until tomorrow.

Slowing down to swing around the corner at the end of the field, she realized that she was actually making plans—thinking well into the future. The past two years had been a grueling day-by-day survival. Totally immersed in the daily obligations, she couldn't see beyond the immediate task; nor did she have the energies to look ahead.

Strange. Her being late last night in picking up the boys because of a stranger's visit seemed to trigger the change. For the first time she realized that the problems she was coping with also troubled the boys. Last night, without giving it serious thought, she promised to stop treating them as babies and to include them in farm and family affairs. Her change in attitude immediately affected them. Even Lexie, who always had to be urged and scolded into doing the simplest tasks, fixed her supper for her without being told.

She remembered the twins' eagerness this morning as they rushed to catch the bus when she told them that the three of them—not she and their grandparents—would have a family conference this evening.

Steering the tractor down the long stretch of the field along the highway, she admitted that it was fun last night to have the boys there during the discussion with the Texan. Thinking about the mystery of the unknown grave and Cotter's own mystery was exciting. As she guided the tractor up and down the quarter-mile lengths of the field, she passed the time thinking about various solutions to the mystery. It was very possible that the woman buried by the tracks was Cotter's relative. His story had more authenticity than any other she ever heard. Perhaps when she got caught up—maybe this winter—she'd see if she could dig up any records. She almost stopped the tractor when she remembered that she didn't know Cotter's address. "Cotter Lewis, Artist, Texas," would hardly find him. Oh, well, he was long gone and the likelihood of her finding out any information to tie the woman to his family was remote.

When she turned around the next time, she spied the yellow bus turning into her gravel road. Without finishing that round, she cut diagonally across the field to the house in anticipation of seeing her sons.

Together they fed the animals. Rainy, not being able to keep up with all of them, settled on trailing Pippa.

"Did you finish disking?" Vance asked. From his vantage point in the open loft door of the old barn, he could see beyond the machinery barn to the field. He pulled off a chunk of the special alfalfa hay reserved for the horses and tossed it out the door for Lexie to carry to them.

"No, not quite. I'll finish tomorrow and then start drilling the wheat. I got a late start. I had to go to town first."

"Get the check?" Vance asked, climbing down the ladder. He removed his ball cap and knocked bits of hay from it. Carefully smoothing down his blond hair, he replaced the cap.

"Yes, sweetie." With both boys anxiously waiting for her to elaborate, she added, "And yes, it was a big one. Better than I hoped for."

"Yeah!" Vance whooped. He then looked at his brother, cocking his head sideways a couple of times toward Pippa to urge him to speak.

"Can we get them new bikes now?" Lexie asked, opening and closing his always-active hands.

Instead of, "You know we can't afford luxuries like that"—words that the boys expected to hear—she said, "We'll see."

Why not? The boys deserved something nice. They'd also had a rather bleak time since their father's death.

"Maybe Christmas," she said, smiling.

The boys exchanged wondering glances at the change in their mother. Behind her back Lexie bent over slightly and brought his fist down in front of him in the victory motion. Vance nodded happily. Both boys grinned, their dimples dancing.

Before she showed any further weakness, Pippa changed the subject. "Looks like the hogs have been rooting again in the shed." She was in the shed of the old barn. The wooden barn had been built in 1868 by a Greenlee ancestor to replace the earlier barn bushwhackers had burned during the Civil War. The shed, added many years later, was attached to the east side of the old barn. Inside the open end of the shed, behind a new, twelve-foot metal gate, Pippa stepped carefully around an area where the ground was churned up. Rainy sniffed the lumps of straw, dirt, and manure. When he started digging vigorously in the hole the hogs had started, Pippa jerked him back by his collar. "Let's keep the gate closed, guys. No need for the hogs to be in here during this mild weather. Lexie, get me a rake and shovel. We better rake this loose dirt back into the hole."

Rainy didn't want to be pulled from his digging. Vance grabbed his collar to deter him. While Lexie went after the tools, Vance said, "We saw that man again."

"What man?"

"The guy who was here last night."

"Yeah," Lexie said, handing her the rake. "From the bus we saw his van parked by the side of the road down east of the house."

"And he was out in our pasture, just standing there looking straight ahead," Vance said.

"Stupid, he was painting," Lexie said, holding an imaginary brush and daubing it on a "picture."

"Painting?"

"Yeah, didn't you see his easel?"

Pippa was both interested and concerned. Interested that the stranger was still around, because this morning when she noticed that his van was gone from his temporary campsite at the crossroads, she assumed that he'd gone back to Texas. She was concerned because, without permission, he was in her pasture with the cattle, though his presence didn't frighten her. His gentle eyes and mild manners—and his easy camaraderie with the boys—caused her to trust him from the beginning.

Just as she started pushing the dirt and muck back into the hole, she heard the familiar thud, followed by a jingle, of Rube butting the gate. "Hello, anyone here?" came a man's deep voice.

"It's that guy!" Lexie said, bolting out of the shed toward the gate to the house. Vance and Pippa followed.

They had neglected to latch the gate and Rube was out. The goat had perfected how to escape if the gate wasn't fastened. She butted the light gate up against its wooden corner post so that it bounced back toward her just open enough that she could catch it with her head and slither through. Cotter had climbed to the top of the board fence, but Rube, reared up on her hind legs, had a firm mouth hold on his pants leg. Struggling to keep his balance, he had a precarious hold on a thin branch of the overhanging maple tree. Even as he teetered on the fence, a cascade of orange leaves fell on him and Rube from the shaking branch.

Lexie was laughing too hard to help, but Vance and Pippa grabbed Rube's horns, one on each side of the irate goat.

"Rube, it's all right," Vance said softly, shaking his head. "He's not going to hurt us."

While Vance pulled on Rube's horns, it took both Pippa and Lexie to force the goat's front legs down from the fence. Lexie yanked a long strip of Cotter's jeans out of her mouth.

"Bad girl, bad girl," Vance scolded, though he was too amused to make his voice strict.

Undaunted, Rube continued to struggle. In spite of her head being firmly held, she managed to lower it into a butting position and pawed the grass with her front feet.

"Did she hurt you?" Pippa asked. She was worried for his safety, furious at the animal, and, like Lexie, laughing. The Texan, with his tooled boots and Stetson hat, did look ridiculous, half over the fence with his white leg gleaming through the long rip in his jeans.

"Only my pride," he said. He carefully climbed back down the fence and fingered his pants. "And a rather damaged pair of jeans."

"I'm so sorry. I don't know what's got into Rube." Pippa watched the twins pushing and pulling Rube toward the old barn. They put her into the shed and securely closed the strong gate. There she could butt all she wanted, for the only thing she could hurt would be herself. But she was too smart to try that here. Long ago she had learned this gate wouldn't give. When the boys left her with admonitions to be good, she stood quietly, though still trembling, eyes sad, and head drooping so low that her thin chin whiskers almost dragged in the straw on the ground.

"She can't understand why we're punishing her for protecting us," Vance said.

"Don't blame her," Cotter said. "It's my fault for coming unannounced. I should know Rube by now." He petted Rainy who was leaning against his ragged pants leg as if to atone for the bad manners of another Greenlee farm inhabitant.

"Vance and I saw you out in our pasture," Lexie said. "What's there to draw out there?"

"Oh, lots of things, Lexie. It's a great place—the beautiful black cattle, the many-colored goats, the creek, the ponds, the autumn trees, flowers, and grasses. At first I was just looking around at all the sights, but when I saw so many varieties of prairie forbs and grasses, I couldn't resist sketching some."

"Huh!" Vance said disparagingly. Grass didn't interest him.

"Are you a botanist?" Pippa asked.

"Yeah, I guess that is part of what I am, a biologist. I have a contract with the University of Oklahoma Press for colored drawings and photographs for a book about prairie plants. I was going to Kansas to research, not realizing that there is so much here."

"Yes, the western border of Missouri was once all prairie," Pippa said.

"I didn't realize that. I'd like to hang around a while. This would be a perfect time to catch the fall blooms."

"Our meadowlands have never been plowed. Actually there's three different pastures so we can move the cattle from one to another. But sprouts and trees were beginning to take it over, so we got some goats to help keep down the brush.''

''They eat anything,'' Lexie said.

''Stuff the cattle won't touch,'' Vance said.

''And even old jeans!'' Lexie teased. Cotter made a face at him.

Ignoring Lexie, Pippa said, ''After grazing a season or two, the goats kill back the sprouts.''

Looking at the rent in his trousers, Cotter said, ''I wondered why you had goats. I admired the herd down in the pasture. They didn't attack me. In fact, they seemed to like me.''

''Rube won't associate with them,'' Lexie said, holding his nose in the air in a haughty manner and imitating the goat's regal movements.

''She likes us better,'' Vance said, laughing at Lexie. ''She always stays up here close to us when we let her.''

''Which we usually do,'' Pippa added. ''The boys enjoy playing with her.''

''Not to mention she guards the place?'' Cotter asked.

''That too.''

''She doesn't know she's a goat.'' Lexie laughed.

''Maybe you should tell her,'' Cotter said.

''And break her heart?'' Pippa asked.

''Hey, want to stay for supper?'' Lexie asked, changing the subject, his face serious and eager. ''We've done the chores and I'll fix us some sandwiches.''

''Yeah!'' Vance said quickly before his mother could intercede. ''Lexie makes good sandwiches. I'll help.'' Though he was speaking to Cotter, his pleading face was turned toward Pippa.

"But your mother—" Cotter started to object.

Pippa smiled. "Please stay."

"Yes, Lexie," Cotter said as he turned to the boy, "I'd love to stay."

"Yeah!" The boys cheered, both grinning in pleasure.

"Cotter," Lexie paused at the kitchen door and asked, "how come you never get me and Vance mixed up? Most people can't tell us apart."

"Easy," Cotter answered, grinning and mussing Lexie's hair. "You have deeper dimples."

"Aw!" Lexie frowned, at first taking him seriously.

Cotter winked at him and patted Vance on his shoulder. "And Vance has about six more freckles than you."

The twins laughed and then headed for the kitchen. Smiling, Pippa and Cotter watched them scramble in and let the door slam shut behind them.

Pippa sat down on the edge of the patio. Just as last night, the evening shadows danced across the yard. The insects harmonized, and a single bobwhite gave its cheery call, followed almost immediately by its mate. "I'm really sorry about your pants."

"They were worn, anyway. I've got another pair in my van."

Neither said anything for a few minutes. He stood near her with his right leg propped up on the patio, looking over the farm. The plaintive whistle of a locomotive grew louder as it gathered speed from climbing the rise out of the river bottom west of Ellis. The short train rolled by, its clamor a sound that belonged there just as did the contented grunts of the pigs and the endless drone of the insects.

After the train disappeared into the east, pulling its rumble with it as it traveled, Cotter spoke in his soft bass. "If you had another hand, you could finish disking and planting that last field tomorrow."

Surprised, Pippa looked up.

"I've been observing," he said.

"Apparently prairie grass wasn't the only thing you noticed."

"Right. I heard in town about your losing your husband." His eyes were kind and sympathetic. "I'm very sorry."

She studied his brown boots, the effects of his tramp in her pasture marring their shine. She did not dare look at his face for fear that the understanding she would find there would bring tears. She murmured the usual reply to sympathy.

"You've done well with the farm," he said.

Pippa was impressed with this quiet man. Most people expressed amazement that a woman alone would even attempt to run a large farm. He seemed to take it as a matter of course.

"As I said," he continued, "if you had help tomorrow, you could finish your fall crop work."

"I'll get it done."

"I assume you plan to plant it in wheat?"

"If I can get it in before another rainy spell, yes. Otherwise, I'll wait until spring and put it back in soybeans or corn."

Cotter stooped over to pull a blade of grass and chewed on it. "I could finish disking while you start planting. With two of us, we could finish tomorrow, or the next day for sure.'' He pushed up the brim of his brown hat to see her reaction.

"We had a hired hand until a couple of months ago. He'd been with us for several years. When he left, I figured I could handle the rest of the harvest—save that extra expense.''

"I don't want any wages. I'll take my pay from permission to use your farm for my work.''

"Heck, you can do that anyway.''

"And there's something else.'' He hesitated as if unsure whether he should say it.

"What's that?''

"Use of your apartment above the equipment barn.''

Pippa stood up in surprise. "You've really cased the place.'' She wasn't sure she was comfortable with this man knowing so much about her place and her plans.

"Not really.'' He seemed to sense her feelings. Before continuing, he took off his hat and ran his fingers through his hair. "You see, this morning I went to the courthouse to see what I could find out about your unknown grave—sheriff records of the inquest, old newspaper reports, you know. Well, I found a dead end. Zilch. *Nada*. In the sheriff's office they looked at me as if I had asked them to resurrect George Washington's false teeth. It seems 1876 is ancient history here—Nothing in any records about a dead woman whom nobody cared about.''

"And the newspaper office?'' She sat down again.

"Same thing. Seems the building burned years ago. There were no records that far back. But everybody I talked to had a different version of this unknown grave. One woman insisted it was a man buried there—some hobo the train ran over.''

"So you didn't get any information to help?"

"No. In fact, the whole story seems more fictional than ever. If it weren't for the solid fact that I've seen the grave out there, I'd think the whole thing is just a myth that has grown over the years."

"Even myths have some basis in fact to start them."

"Yes, that's what I thought. So I went back to the guy from the historical society I talked to yesterday— the one who gave me directions to your place."

"Yes, I know him. I've done business with him." She didn't tell him that the business was to buy a burial monument two years ago. The memory of that ordeal stirred up the latent ache.

"Well, he seemed pretty confident that the story you told me was the correct one. Fifty years or so ago he talked with several old people who were in this neighborhood at the time of the murder."

He paused. From inside the kitchen they heard a loud discussion between the boys. When Cotter started to go in, Pippa held up her hand for him to stay. "Let them handle it," she said. They heard a sound of a dish breaking and several pans falling to the floor. Freewill dashed out of the kitchen. Realizing that the noise didn't hurt him, he calmed down. First he rubbed against Pippa's back, and then stepped into her lap. With his front paws on her shoulder, he rubbed his head against her neck. She stroked him.

Since there was no more commotion from the kitchen, Cotter relaxed and sat down on the patio, holding his hat in his lap.

"The historical society man told me all about you. I didn't ask, but I was glad to hear. So you see, I'm not really nosy, nor did I pry. He just told me. I couldn't avoid listening without being rude. He even told me about the empty apartment for your hired hand.''

Neither said anything. Freewill purred. Rainy, lying at Pippa's feet, suddenly had an urge to scratch his underbelly. The barnyard animals were unusually quiet, except for Rube's restless movements from the old shed.

''So,'' Cotter said, ''I thought, if you were willing, that I could bunk in your apartment for a while so I could do my drawing and photography work, and pay you back by helping on the farm.''

''The apartment goes with the job.''

''I wouldn't want any pay. It'd just be temporary.''

When she didn't answer, he added, ''I was raised on a farm in eastern Texas, land about like this here. I know about crops and machinery and animals.''

Freewill, not satisfied with just Pippa's caresses, was investigating Cotter. Cotter picked him up. Pippa was amazed that the cat didn't struggle to be put down as he usually did.

''What do you say?'' he asked.

Before Pippa could answer, the boys tromped out, grinning proudly, to announce that supper was ready. At their sudden appearance, Freewill jumped down and scurried back through the open door into the house.

The adults entered the kitchen to see the table set with the good china, glasses, and silverware. Pippa hoped that the crash she heard was not one of her good pieces of china. On each of the four plates rested a fat sandwich, with pickles, olives, and chips beside it. Above the fork at each place was a salad bowl filled with lettuce and big chunks of carrots, celery, and tomatoes. Spoiling the elegance of the setting was an opened jar of mustard with a grimy knife stuck into it, a gooey bottle of ketchup, and four different kinds of salad dressings still in their bottles.

The boys waited anxiously to get their mother's approving smile. "This is fine, guys." She hugged first Lexie and then drew Vance into her embrace. "And very pretty. Now let's eat." In a softer voice she said to the twins, "Afterward we have some business with Cotter that the Greenlee partners have to attend to."

Vance's eyes danced as he looked at his mother and then Lexie.

"Way to go!" Lexie said, grabbing his sandwich, and without waiting for the others, took a huge bite.

Chapter Four

V ance and Lexie did most of the talking during the
meal. A few questions from Cotter kept them going.
He listened attentively to everything they said. Before
they finished eating, the boys had told him most of
their life story. He learned that Lexie wanted to be a
baseball player; Vance was more inclined toward track.
Lexie read lots of books, especially adventure and mysteries; Vance preferred being outside, tramping around
the farm or playing with the animals.

"I'll wash the dishes," Cotter offered when there
was nothing left to eat.

"No," Pippa said, "you're company."

"After three times, you're not company, and then
you can help," Lexie said.

"Leave them for now," Pippa said, rising from her
seat and moving into the living room. "We'll do them
later." When everyone was seated again—even Freewill followed them in from the kitchen—she continued,
"Guys, Cotter has a proposition for us. I didn't answer
because we need to decide together."

The boys looked at each other, grinning. They wholeheartedly approved of their mother's new attitude.

"Cotter suggested that . . . no, Cotter you tell them."

"Lexie and Vance, you and your mother have some things that I'd like to use, and I think that I can pay for them by helping. I've offered to help your mother finish that west field, and other jobs later, with no pay, in return for being allowed to draw and photograph the plants in your pastures. And, since my van isn't too comfortable, especially now that it's getting colder, I'd like to bunk in your apartment out in the machinery barn."

Lexie started to agree immediately, but Vance poked him and gave him a warning glance not to appear too eager. Businessmen didn't jump into things, but studied all angles.

"What do you think, guys?" their mother asked.

"Sounds good to—" Lexie started to say.

Vance interrupted him. "What do you know about driving a tractor?"

"I've plowed and disked and planted on my parents' farm ever since I wasn't much older than you."

"We can drive the little tractor," Lexie said, not to be outdone.

Vance studied Cotter before asking his next question. "How can you help Mom if you're doing your thing with the plants?"

"I'll help her get the wheat planted before I start. I can do my work at odd times. I'll put the farm work first."

"Doesn't seem right that we don't pay you," Lexie said.

"Yeah." Vance nodded vigorously. "We always paid guys that worked for us unless Daddy traded work."

"I agree with the boys," Pippa said. "We can't possibly ask you to work without paying you."

"Right," Vance said.

"Yeah," Lexie agreed, emphasizing his opinion with his hand movements.

"Well, we have a standoff," Cotter said. "I've got the job if you pay me, is that it?"

The three Greenlees looked at one another and then nodded. "We can't expect you to work for nothing, not being a relative or a close friend or neighbor we can trade work with," Pippa said.

"I understand," Cotter said with disappointment. He thought for a moment. "So let's compromise. I'll help get that last field planted just for the use of your place, but after that, I'll take what you paid your last hand. Okay?"

When the twins both nodded enthusiastically, Pippa agreed.

Suddenly Vance put his hand to his opened mouth. "What about Rube?"

"Stupid goat," Lexie said.

"She's not stupid. She's smarter than you."

"Is not."

"Is too."

Pippa put a stop to their bickering. "You guys stop that. Vance is right. Rube is smart and she does pose a problem. She seems to have taken a dislike to you, Cotter. We can't have her treeing you all the time."

"Yeah," Lexie said, "we might run out of fences for you to climb."

Pippa gave him a warning glance to watch it and then said to the boys, "I suppose we could keep her shut up until she gets used to him."

"I'll watch out for her and be careful not to come upon her unexpectedly like I did tonight," Cotter said. "I'll make friends with her. I've never met an animal that I couldn't get along with." Evidence of that was Freewill climbing into his lap. Cotter scratched the ecstatic cat under his chin with both hands. "How did Rube get to be such a character? There must be a story about her, because she is so different from those goats in your herd down in the pasture."

"Yes, there's a story," Pippa said, her eyes snapping in fun.

"Tell me. I need to know what I'm up against."

"Just the highlights, or the whole story?"

"The whole works," Cotter said, when he saw the anticipation on the twins' faces for one of their mother's stories.

"The boys probably don't remember much of this. We got Rube, let's see"—she stopped to think—"six years ago."

"We were just four then," Vance said, moving to the couch to sit next to Pippa. As he leaned against his mother, she put her arm around him.

"You never told us," Lexie said, stretching out on the floor at her feet on his stomach. He waited for her to begin with his chin cupped in his hands, elbows anchored in the rug.

Three expectant faces turned toward her. During her first few sentences she addressed Cotter since he asked for the story, but she soon faced the boys when their father became part of the action. She began:

"One evening about six years ago, I was surprised to see Rube Nelson and her boy. They bumped down our drive in their old topless jalopy. Its fenders were red, but the rest of the ancient car was bright yellow with signs and pictures painted all over it. You know I don't know cars, Vance, but it was a Ford, probably about a 1950 model.

"This was the first time I had any dealings with Cal Nelson's family, though I had seen them and been by their place. The neighbors referred to them as river rats. They used to live in an ugly log hut down in the river bottom. The dirt yard was bordered in front by a split-log fence, the poles standing upright side by side. A cot, stove, tricycle, broken wagon, discarded kitchen utensils, pigs, chickens, and kids were scattered haphazardly. Close to the house were a few smaller log buildings. A well-worn path led across the little clearing to the river. There was a log barn slightly removed from the other buildings. We heard that Cal's daughter Rube and her boy had a fight with the old man and lived in the barn—it looked to me to be about as habitable as the house.

"Cal was shiftless and produced a big family of kids like himself. However, they knew more about woodcraft than any of their neighbors. Old Cal and his sons could handle an ax in the woods better than anyone in the area. They knew all about timber, wildlife, and fish. A Nelson rarely went hunting or fishing without success, in season or out, it made no difference. Excellent marksmen, craftsmen, and woodcutters, they would work only long enough to earn money for ammunition or a new pair of jeans.

"When Cal was old enough to receive SSI checks, he stopped working. His sons worked less also since the family had a steady income sufficient for their needs. If we could catch him in the right humor—or more likely, if he liked us—we could get him to make fence posts, make a split-oak basket, a child's chair, an ax handle. He could make anything, using the resources of the woodsy river bottom where he squatted. He charged very little for his work and often did it for nothing—if we could get him to do it.

"Now boys, your daddy knew the Nelsons all his life, having gone to school with the younger children when they attended. Apparently he stood high in old Cal's estimation, for Cal often made hammer handles for him and charged only a few cents.

"Generally the neighborhood ignored the Nelsons, going to them only at busy seasons when trying to hire extra hands. (I had lived near them for six years and never been close enough to speak.) They wanted to be left alone because they were self-sufficient, independent, and contented in their crude house built on a neighbor's land.

"Naturally I was curious when Cal's daughter Rube and her boy drove up. The boy's face was broken out, and while he talked he never looked up but stared at his dirty hands grasping the steering wheel as if I was going to wrest it away from him. Under her chin, Rube had tied a kerchief which stuck out from her head, half concealing her flat face. She kept her eyes straight forward, letting the boy do all the talking.

" 'Hello,' I said. I had to walk out to the driveway

since they made no effort to leave their car. 'Won't you get out?' I asked when I got no response to my greeting.

" 'Your man about?' the boy asked, ignoring my invitation.

" 'He's out back. I'll go get him.'

"Daddy was astonished when I told him who our visitors were. 'What do they want?' he asked, half expecting trouble. I shrugged and followed him back to where they sat motionless just as I left them.

" 'Hi,' Daddy said. 'What can I do for you?'

" 'Wanna buy a goat?' the boy asked, turning toward him, almost sighing in his relief to talk business with a man.

" 'Hadn't thought much about it,' Daddy said. 'You got one to sell?'

"The boy nodded his head. 'A four-year-old nanny. We're movin' and want to get rid of her.'

" 'What'll you take for her?' Daddy asked. I was surprised he was even interested. We did want some goats, brush goats, to keep down the sprouts and underbrush, but we weren't ready yet because we didn't have a woven wire fence all around the pasture, a necessity to hold goats. Besides, what good would one lone goat be on three hundred acres of pasture?

" 'I'll take fifteen fer 'er,' Rube's boy said.

" 'I'll give you ten,' Daddy said. If someone drove up selling an ostrich, Daddy would have bid on it and bought it if he got a good trade. I didn't pay much attention to the bargaining. I knew, as did Daddy and the boy, that they would eventually compromise in the middle. Each tried to hold his own, giving a little each time until they agreed.

"Every time the boy dropped his price he glanced at his mother. She made no sign she even heard the discussion, but apparently gave some indication of approval, for the boy continued. When Daddy offered twelve-fifty as his top price the boy and his mother conferred silently again and agreed to take it.

" 'You bring her over,' Daddy said.

" 'I'll bring 'er 'round tomorry,' the boy said, then tried to start his car. It sputtered and choked a few times. Just when I thought we'd have to push them to get them off the place, the engine caught and the jalopy sputtered down the drive, Rube's red scarf flopping out from her head as she sat stiff and straight in the seat.

"While I was doing the evening chores the next day, I heard their old Ford sputter up the drive again. The boy and Rube looked as if they hadn't moved since the day before, the boy staring at the steering wheel and Rube's scarf half concealing her face.

"But from the open backseat directly behind the boy, a big, white woolly goat stood erect with her head high. The rectangular pupils in her intelligent brown eyes met mine. She was the only one of the trio in the car who ever looked directly at me. Inquisitively she examined you boys and me as we stared back at her. Her silky white wool hung in perfect ringlets almost to the tattered seat she was standing on. Like a queen, she posed, dignified and at ease, while the two attendants in front drove her about the country. I had a terrible desire to sweep off my straw hat, bow, and say, 'This way, milady.'

"As before the couple held their ground after they stopped. This time Daddy wasn't home. With difficulty

I kept a straight face, turning from the goat to the people in front.

"I told the boy to drive around to the barn lot and put the goat in the shed. He drove his jalopy around the house and took the goat's rope from his mother's hand to lead her into the shed. The goat leaped easily out of the car and followed the boy into the shed with short, dainty steps. When free of the rope she turned to continue her scrutiny of us.

" 'She'll stay about the house once she takes up with you,' Rube said. Sill rooted in her seat in the car she continued to stare straight ahead. Her voice startled me. I'd almost believed her mute.

" 'We don't have any fence to hold her,' I ventured, to carry on the conversation.

" 'Ain't used to none.'

"No, I guessed she wasn't. In her former home she probably went through the open, screenless doors of the house whenever she wanted. She probably slept in the kitchen from the looks of her beautiful wool and her bulging sides.

" 'We were wondering if she'd take up with the cows. We thought if she did she wouldn't try to get out so much until we build a good fence.'

" 'She won't leave.'

"When I paid the boy, he volunteered, 'Sold ten dollars worth of wool off 'er last spring.'

"After being so loquacious they drove off, leaving us to get acquainted with the goat. I had forgotten to ask her name. No matter. We promptly called her Queen Rube.

"Since it was almost dark, I tore myself from the goat to go after the cattle. The herd wasn't as big then, and we liked to feed them up here each night to keep better tabs on them. I had no difficulty starting them home. They walked in front of me single file to the barn lot, anxious for their feed. All at once a cowbell clanged and Babe—we'd just got her, boys, and she was really timid then—Babe ran awkwardly back to the pasture, her eyes bugged out in fright, her bag swinging from side to side, and her little black calf trotting behind. The other cows and calves were right behind her. The horses were prancing around as if they'd seen a snake. Then I spotted what scared the animals. The goat, Rube, was parading regally around the barn lot claiming her new kingdom. Daddy had come home while I was getting the cows, and discovering the goat, had turned her loose to see what she would do. He didn't think about her scaring the stock.

" 'Hey!' I hollered, trying to head off the cattle. 'Get that goat out of sight if you want these cows in the lot tonight.' By running back and forth in front of them, yelling, and brandishing my stick, I stopped their stampede but couldn't drive them back to the barnyard until Daddy put Rube in the hog lot out of sight.

"The other cows soon became accustomed to Rube, but it was weeks before Babe would venture near her. We kept Rube in the hog lot for a time, but she always stayed as close to the barnyard gate as she could get while in the lot. Even though there was a twelve-foot gate between them, Babe wouldn't enter the shed to be fed until we put Rube out of sight.

"After a few months, when even Babe ignored her, we turned Rube out with the cattle. We didn't have to worry about our lack of goat-proof fence, because once we convinced her she couldn't stay in the lawn, and most certainly not in the house, she left the barn lot only once each day to go to the pasture to graze her fill of the brush and sprouts.

"She became quite a pet. Vance, even then you could catch her anytime you wanted and lead her around or jump on her broad back for a ride, just as you do now. Though she bossed and butted the cows, hogs, and dogs when they got in her way, she never butted you guys. She submitted meekly to anything you wanted. Sometimes, Lexie, you treated her pretty rough, pulling on her wool, hitching her up to all kinds of contraptions. She never objected.

"The next spring when the days grew warm, Rube would lie in the shade panting. Her long, heavy wool began to come off on fences and posts where she rubbed. Her horns were usually full of wool from scratching herself to get rid of her heavy coat.

"One hot, late April day Daddy sheared her. He clipped off all the wool he could and finished the job with electric clippers. When he got through, she was half her usual size and naked down to her pink skin. A more comfortable, but ridiculous-looking, goat walked around the lot. Freed of her heavy coat, she walked gracefully about with delicate steps, her dignified head high as usual, like a queen. However, she looked as if she had on long underwear.

"That very night it turned cold again, remaining chilly for several days. Poor Rube shivered and seldom ventured from the farthermost corner of the shed except when the sun shone brightly in the middle of the day. Vance, you tried to put one of your old sweaters on her, but she would have nothing to do with that. That's when Freewill and she became good friends. Freewill was just a kitten then, but he would make a comfortable bed on top of her when she lay basking in the sun, her head turned back against her back legs.

"We all agreed that Rube wasn't a goat but a species all her own. She certainly didn't act like a goat. After we had her for a year we built a goat-proof fence and bought a few nannies and kids. Rube merely looked at these intruders, turned her back to them, and lay down by the old barn to chew her cud. We put her in the shed with the new goats to see what she would do. Penned up with the lowly creatures, she soon showed them their place in the farm pecking order. Twice the size of even the older nannies, she butted them all into a corner and kept watch over them. Whenever one left the corner she butted it back.

"After a couple of hours of that we turned them out. Once she was free, Rube had nothing more to do with these lowly goats. They stayed in the pasture, feasting on the tender sprouts, but she continued to spend most of her time in the barnyard where she could see everything that happened to us, her real family, and enjoy the feel of Freewill's warm body on her back as she dozed in the sun on winter days."

Chapter Five

After Cotter left and Pippa and Lexie were clearing the table, Vance went outside to check on the animals and let Rube out of the shed. He came back in carrying something in his hand.

"Whatcha got?" Lexie asked, trying to get at Vance, who dodged him.

"Just an old bone." He quickly stuck it under his dirty sweatshirt.

"Lemme see."

"No. It's mine. I found it." The boys began scuffling until Pippa stopped them.

"But Vance won't let me see his bone." Lexie pouted.

"Show it to him," Pippa ordered. Wiping off the table, she was preoccupied with analyzing her feelings. She had for the first time since Doug's death talked about him easily and naturally without pain. In fact, she had told an amusing story which included him. She felt good, sort of cleansed in a way. Remembering his experiences with Rube let loose a flood of good memories without exposing the aching void. Instead of having to swallow a sob, she was almost smiling.

"I don't see why I have to," Vance said, holding his arms over his chest to prevent Lexie from snatching his bone. "I want to take it to school tomorrow for show-and-tell in science period. If I let him see it, Lexie will spoil it like he always does by telling everyone beforehand."

Vance's words only half penetrated her thoughts. She didn't want this argument to ruin her good mood or interrupt her train of thought. She was wrong about being alone anymore. The boys' taking on responsibility and entering into the business deal with Cotter proved that.

And Cotter himself? Part of the reason she was so relaxed tonight was knowing she had help tomorrow. For the first time in several months she didn't worry whether she could get everything done. She wouldn't dread getting out of bed in the morning to face another day.

Cotter seemed a perfect answer. She couldn't afford a full-time hand, and part-time help was almost impossible to get, besides being undependable. Here he came, volunteering for just what she needed. Nice too— friendly, unassuming, understanding. Handsome. The boys liked him. So did Rainy and Freewill. But not Rube. Oh, well, the goat was a minor problem. Pippa remembered her mother saying once that a man both dogs and children liked was a good man. That was good enough recommendation for her.

It was pleasant having someone her own age visit them. For months only people her parents' age or the twins' friends had been in the house. Still smiling, she punched the button to start the dishwasher. Turning around, she bumped into Vance standing stubbornly behind her.

"Why do I have to?" he asked. His lower lip was turned down. He intended to stand his ground.

Pippa brought her attention back to him. Oh, yes. Something about a bone he found. As parents she and Doug had always made an effort to treat each of the twins individually, to encourage their differences. They gave them dissimilar names, never dressed them alike, and did not always include them as a pair. Here she was forcing Vance to give in to his brother as if being his twin gave Lexie that right. Bad move, even though the easiest way to stop their bickering was to make Vance give in to his more determined brother. *Got to watch that,* she told herself.

"You're right, Vance. You don't have to show Lexie."

Vance was still hiding the bone under his shirt. As proof of his right, she didn't ask to see it either, but she could tell that it was a long, narrow one—probably a leg bone from a deer Rainy found killed along the railroad. "Where did you find it?"

"In the shed. Rube was digging in that hole by the gate the hogs started."

"Probably one Rainy buried. Remind me to finish filling it tomorrow," Pippa said.

"Don't want to see your stupid ol' bone," Lexie taunted. "Rainy has bones buried all over the place."

"This one's different," Vance said.

"Okay, that's enough." Pippa's voice was firm. "Get to bed now." As they started upstairs grumbling, she called after them, her voice tender, "Lexie, Vance,

I think we made the right decision tonight about Cotter.''

"Yeah, we did," Vance said. Lexie nodded.

"He asked me this afternoon, but I wasn't sure what to tell him until I knew what you guys thought."

Their squabble over the bone forgotten, the boys grinned at each other. They made the high-five sign and raced up the stairs.

From the tractor cab the next afternoon, as she swung wide to begin another row with the wheat drill, Pippa watched Cotter complete the final round with the disk. He was about halfway across the field from her by the highway. Jumping down from the tractor, he seemed to be looking for something on the ground. She thought something was wrong, until she noticed his camera.

She felt good about him. He had waited until he was finished before using her time to take pictures. She watched him kneel on the ground, his camera to his eye. He switched lenses and focused her way. She was too far away to tell if he was using a telephoto lens, but since he was facing her, she waved. Yes, he had a powerful lens. He waved back.

Smiling to herself, she surveyed the level expanse of smoothed-out, black soil in front of her that Cotter had prepared. Taking the tractor out of gear and pausing before she made another turn, she rested her arms on the steering wheel. The moisture content of the soil was perfect, dry enough for the dirt not to clod, but damp enough to sprout the seed. A perfect seedbed.

Pleased with their progress and Cotter's expertise, she watched him climb back on his tractor and circle back toward the buildings. Good. He had worked steadily all morning. She couldn't have covered more ground herself. She started down the new row. Into the seedbed behind her, the wheat drill was dropping kernels and fertilizer in rows about seven inches apart. She checked her watch. They could easily finish, now that she could work more steadily without so many delays. Cotter was free to help her periodically refill the drill.

She scanned the sky. Still no sign of bad weather and the guy on the radio in her cab just announced that the rain would probably hold off for two more days. She sighed with relief. Another crop year as good as completed.

With her back to the house as she headed south down the long row, she didn't notice the activity there until she turned back. Standing beside his tractor, Cotter was photographing her as she drew near him. He had stopped to wait for her at the end of the row nearest the buildings.

"What's up?" Cotter asked, pointing to the driveway. "What's the commotion at the house? You expecting anybody?"

Pippa turned to see two official-looking white cars parked in the drive. There were some men standing on the lawn and one on the porch. Apparently one of the men just noticed her, for he pointed his arm in her direction. The man on the porch stepped back onto the lawn.

Her stomach lurched. "Oh, that's the sheriff." Then panic momentarily stopped her. "Something's wrong." Her first thought was the boys, followed immediately by the fear that something had happened to one of her parents. Then a bizarre thought occurred to her that maybe Cotter was a fugitive. Did she know for sure he was who he said he was? Banishing that idea, she jumped down out of the tractor cab and started walking toward the house.

Thinking better of it, she said, "I'll take your tractor to the house to see."

"Shall I come in?" Cotter asked as she took his seat.

"No. You take over the drill. Keep on working. I'll let you know. Probably it's nothing." He immediately crawled into the big tractor cab and headed it across the field at a crawl. Did she expect to see him sneaking out and fleeing? Silly thought.

As she drew near the buildings, the men—she counted four of them—all stood together awaiting her arrival.

"Are you Mrs. Greenlee?" one of them asked as soon as she climbed down from the tractor and stepped through the barnyard gate onto the back lawn. Pippa knew he was the sheriff from his picture on the election posters. She quieted Rainy, and tried to ignore Rube's restless pacing behind the fence.

"Yes. Is there any trouble?"

"Well, no, but we got to check out something."

"Oh." Relief flooded her. The boys were all right. She tightened her grip on Rainy's collar to restrain his angry lunges. "What do you mean, check out something?" Did they think she was growing marijuana or making whiskey? Then she thought again about Cotter. Maybe he was the one they were checking out!

The men exchanged embarrassing glances. "Well," the sheriff said, "we got a report that there was a body buried here."

"Oh! You must mean the unknown grave." Not

Cotter either. She was surprised how relieved she was. She smiled. "It's over there across the road in the weeds by the tracks."

The sheriff's solemn expression didn't change. "No, not that one. Another one. Out in your barn."

"My barn . . . you must be mistaken. There's nothing buried out there." Then she understood and laughed—the deer bone that Vance found. Of course. It was big enough to look like a human bone. "You mean that deer bone that my son found in the barn last night?"

When the sheriff nodded, she said, "We have lots of animals here, wild and domesticated. Sometimes they die. My dog here buries them. What's so unusual about that?"

Rube was butting the gate repeatedly with increasing force.

When the sheriff still didn't change his expression, she asked, worried again, looking at the other men who all had equally serious faces. "And how'd you learn about Vance's bone, anyway?"

"Well, Mrs. Greenlee, it seems the bone is not an animal bone, but a human bone." The sheriff let this fact sink in. "When your boy showed it in science this morning, his teacher, Bob Cunningham, recognized it as a human arm bone—a left ulna to be exact. He called me."

"Couldn't be human. He must have been mistaken."

"No mistake. He knows human bones. He went to medical school a couple of years."

To Pippa this was like some novel she was reading—

it couldn't actually be happening. Too weird. She had to say something. "Did you see it?"

"Not yet. I sent a man to the school for it and came straight out here." Though the sheriff's accusing eyes were about to mesmerize her, she didn't look away. He was almost gruff in his manner, but Pippa tried to speak normally.

"You think there's been a murder committed here?" She couldn't believe she was saying this line that belonged in a bad television script. And her manner of saying it! A director would fire her for bad acting, but she wasn't acting at all. She couldn't help the way she was reacting to this crazy situation.

"Yes." The sheriff's definite answer and stern, unflinching look frightened Pippa. This was no TV show. She was genuinely frightened. Were they going to arrest her?

"Who's that out in the field?" he asked, pointing to Cotter.

"My new hand." *Oh, please God, not Cotter,* she prayed.

"I'll send one of my men after him." The sheriff motioned to his deputy, who started to leave.

"No need," Pippa said, putting out her hand to stop the deputy, but not touching him. "I'll get him in." Dragging Rainy after her by his collar, and hoping that the gate would hold Rube, Pippa hurried to the west fence and waved both hands over her head to attract Cotter's attention. He blinked the tractor lights several times to acknowledge he saw her. She figured that he would be watching the activity at the house and would understand her signal. They all watched as he immediately unhitched the drill and cut across the field as fast as his tractor could go.

"Where did the boy find the bone?" the sheriff asked.

After first dragging Rube into a closed-in stall in the old barn and latching the door securely on the furious goat, Pippa then led the men to the shed. The rake and shovel, both covered with the muck of the shed floor, were lying forgotten on the ground near the hole where she had dropped them last night when Cotter showed up.

"The hogs rooted out this hole, and last night when we penned our goat in here she dug some more," she said. The hole was bigger and deeper, showing evidence of Rube's pawing. As soon as the shed gate was open, Rainy ran in and began digging furiously with both front paws. Pippa pulled him back. He struggled out of her grasp. With a piece of rope she found hanging from a nail on the shed wall, she tied him to one of the rungs of the gate out of reach of the hole and the men. He howled until Pippa's firm voice made him be quiet. His whimpering and moaning, and an occasional howl he couldn't control, accompanied the booms of Rube's head on attacks of the partition between the barn stall and the shed.

"Your animals aren't very friendly," one of the deputies said. Pippa thought the same about the sheriff and his men.

Just then Cotter ran up to them. "What's going on?" he asked, worried, looking from Pippa to the men.

"There's been a body buried here, probably murdered," the sheriff said dramatically, walking around the site and studying it carefully.

The sheriff sounded so melodramatic that Cotter looked to Pippa to see if he was in earnest. Pippa stepped close to him and nodded. They stood close together away from the men, her hand clutching his arm. He patted her hand.

"After you left last night, Vance found a bone here that Rube dug up, and he took it to school. We thought it was a deer bone," Pippa explained softly. "Seems it turns out to be human."

"You can't possibly suspect Mrs. Greenlee. . . ." Cotter began, very agitated.

Ignoring his outburst, and still inspecting the site, the sheriff said calmly, "No, not now." His manner changed abruptly after his examination of the hole. He now spoke in a pleasant, almost friendly voice. "Except for this surface disturbance, which Mrs. Greenlee says was done by her animals"—he stooped to push aside a clod of dirt—"and the evidence seems to bear that out. See these hoof marks here of the goat and the typical hog rooting signs?" Rube's continual battering of the wall gave audible evidence to his statements. "Except for that, this ground hasn't been disturbed recently. Not in years."

"Of course not," Cotter said. "What did you think?"

"Nothing, Mr. . . . ."

"Lewis, Cotter Lewis."

"Mr. Lewis, I had no suspicions. We got a report that a human bone was found buried in a barn. Had to investigate right away."

The radio in the sheriff's car blared. One of the deputies went to answer it. "Preliminary report from the lab says this bone is over a hundred years old, probably a hundred and twenty,'' he reported when he returned. "Male, Caucasian, about twenty to thirty years old.''

His face flushed with anger, Cotter confronted the sheriff. "You could have waited for that report before you came around scaring Mrs. Greenlee and suggesting she had anything to do with a murder.''

Ignoring Cotter and continuing to study the ground, the sheriff said, "Sorry, Mrs. Greenlee, if we troubled you.'' His voice was not very apologetic as he proceeded to his next task. "But we still have to investigate. I've got a warrant to search your place. But do I have your permission to dig some more here to see what we find?''

This was new ground for Pippa, who had never had any experience with the law. She automatically looked to Cotter for advice. He returned to her side, took her hand, and nodded. Under the anger, Pippa thought she detected a growing excitement in his face that began with the deputy's report about the identity of the bone. But so inured was she to her work schedule, all she could think of was that this emergency, now downgraded to a nuisance, was interfering with her planting. Oh, well. It would be an easy job to finish tomorrow.

The sheriff's men produced picks and shovels and took turns digging. It was hard work, for the ground was packed tight from years of animal hooves pacing and stomping in the shed. The men carefully shoveled out the dirt, which they put on a tarp, searching through each load for bones or other evidence as to the identity of the body. They scooped out a four-foot square down to the level of the deepest place Rube had pawed. At that level they found another long arm bone, then some smaller ones. Even Pippa could recognize them as human finger bones. Wearing plastic gloves, the men put the bones in labelled bags.

"Shouldn't you have someone here that knows how to excavate?" Cotter asked excitedly.

"This is a police investigation, not an archeological dig. We are getting the evidence. Our lab, or the state forensics lab, will tell us what we need to know about this fellow," the sheriff said. He was getting annoyed at Cotter hanging over every move. "Don't you have work to do? Like finish planting that field for this lady?"

Cotter looked at Pippa for instructions. "Can you tell us any more today about who this is?" she asked the sheriff.

"Probably not. We'll dig him up and then fill the hole back for you nice and neat. No need to look anywhere else on the place. From the evidence we find we may learn how he came to be buried here. I don't reckon you know anything in the history of this farm to account for him?"

Pippa shook her head. "I never heard anything."

"No call for you to hang around, then," the sheriff said.

Pippa whispered to Cotter, "What do you think?"

"I think one of us should stay here. I'll go back to the field if you want."

Pippa knew that he didn't want to leave. The excitement in his face was mounting.

"A hundred and twenty years ago would be in the 1870s, wouldn't it?" he asked her.

"Do you think it's. . . . " She cocked her head toward the road.

"The unknown woman's missing man? Got to be," he whispered back.

"You should stay in case they find something besides bones. They may not notice or pay any attention."

"Okay," Cotter agreed quickly. He unconsciously tapped his Nikon hanging on a strap over his shoulder to indicate that he would also take some pictures.

Pippa was torn whether to return to the field or stay. After all, this was her farm. Finding a hundred-year-old body was not an ordinary event. She should see it out. But the wheat? Her work timetable urged her to get it done. Then, after the seed was safely in the ground so that it could sprout to cover and protect the soil's nakedness for the winter, she could give her complete attention to this grave situation.

The field won out. After telling Cotter to send the boys out to the field to her the moment they got home—she wanted them to hear about the sheriff's visit from her—she returned to the field.

For the rest of the afternoon, every row when she faced the buildings, she watched the activity at the old barn shed. Each time she stopped by the loaded pickup parked at the edge of the field to refill the wheat drill from bags of seed and fertilizer, she debated whether to continue or go to the house. She always continued.

After several hours, the men finished and finally loaded the sturdy brown plastic bags containing the bones into the trunks of the cars. They backed out the drive, just before the school bus turned into her gravel road.

Cotter immediately brought the boys to the field. To tell the boys and to bring Pippa up to date, all four of them crammed into the tractor cab so Pippa could continue planting. Only a few more rows to go and she would be finished.

The boys were wild with worry and excitement. Though Mr. Cunningham, their teacher, had said nothing to Vance about his bone, except to ask to keep it, on the bus coming home the high school kids were full of rumors about a dead body. Maybe even a murder! When the twins saw the sheriff's cars on their road, and Cotter there to meet them instead of their mother, they were beside themselves with worry. Cotter quickly allayed their fears, pointing out Pippa in the tractor.

"What happened?" they asked.

"Let's go to your mother. Let her tell you."

After Pippa described the afternoon's events to them, Vance said, "It's all my fault."

"No, Vance, sweetie. Why do you say that?"

"If I hadn't taken that old bone to school, no one would have ever known."

"No, don't think that. It's a good thing you did. We sure don't want a dead body buried in our shed. Besides"—she paused and looked at Cotter—"Cotter and I think that this body may be a clue in the unknown grave mystery."

Lexie's eyes got big. "That he's the man with the unknown woman?" he asked.

"That's a possibility," Cotter said.

"And I've helped solve a murder?" Vance asked, brightening up.

"Could be you've found a clue to help solve it," Pippa said. "So far it's only another mystery."

"Wow! Now there's two ghosts haunting our house!" Lexie said gleefully.

Pippa groaned as she looked at Cotter with a what-do-I-do-with-him look. She maneuvered the tractor to start the last section of the field. Now that the boys were satisfied, she asked Cotter, "What happened after I left? I thought the men would never leave."

"They uncovered an entire skeleton. When they saw that, they worked very carefully. The dead guy measured about five feet, eight inches. He was lying on his right side, as if dumped into the hole and hastily covered with dirt. That's why the topmost bone, the one Rube dug up and you found, Vance, was a left arm bone. They found the bones of that arm sort of scattered, but when they reached the shoulder and hips and the rest of the body, the skeleton was intact, though not straightened out as would have been done in a regular burial."

"There was a skeleton lying there in the shed all the time?" Lexie was squirming so much in the crowded cab that Cotter had to hold him to keep him from bumping Pippa's driving arm.

"For about a hundred and twenty years, so it seems," Cotter said.

"Cool!" Lexie said. "Wait till I tell the class tomorrow."

"You can't tell," Vance said. "I found the arm bone. I get to tell." They started pushing each other.

Pippa stopped the tractor. "You both get out right now. I can't have this continual fussing."

"We won't fuss," Lexie promised, subdued.

"We'll both tell it in school." Vance begged, "We want to hear what else Cotter has to say." They both promised to remain very still if they didn't have to leave.

Cotter stroked his beard as he continued. "When the men finally removed all the dirt from around the skeleton—that was what took so much time—they discovered that the man really had been murdered. There was some lead from a shotgun, probably a twelve-gauge, lodged in the skull. The forehead was shattered, as if he was shot at close range."

"A murder in our barn!" Vance's excitement mounted. "And I discovered it."

"Way cool!" Lexie said.

"Anything else?" Pippa asked, almost as excited as the boys.

"The whole body was pretty well preserved, being in the barn out of the wet and weather all the time. The clothing was all gone, but there was a metal belt buckle and some buttons, probably from his coat. But nothing to help identify him—no initials or insignia."

"Do you still think it could be that Herb guy that your Ivy ran off with?" Pippa asked.

"More than ever. Right age, right number of years ago. Two graves so close together. Too much of a coincidence."

"Did you say anything to the sheriff about your suspicions?"

"No, and he didn't make any connection with the two graves. Since the murder happened so long ago, he wasn't too concerned. He won't have to investigate it, but said he would run all he has through the forensics lab. I asked him to do all he could to find out anything more because you would want to know as a historical fact for your farm. He may come up with something else."

"I'll see what I can find out about which Greenlee

owned the farm back then,'' Pippa said. ''There's a bunch of papers and photographs in the old dresser in the north room. I'll go through them. Maybe I'll find something. The boys can help, since it's their ancestors that lived here.''

''I'll help,'' Lexie said. ''I'm the best reader.''

''Are not.''

''Am too.''

Ignoring their argument, Cotter asked them, ''Lexie, Vance, can you keep our secret?''

They both frowned in disappointment, so eager were they to tell at school all these exciting events on their farm. None of their friends ever discovered a murdered body—a real skeleton in their closet—uh, barn.

Pippa said, ''Just the part about us thinking maybe this man had something to do with our unknown grave and Cotter's connection to it. You can tell everything else. Then if we find out there really is a connection to the grave, you guys can tell everyone.''

''Okay?'' Cotter asked.

''Yeah, sure,'' Lexie said happily.

''We won't tell,'' Vance agreed, proud to be included again in the adult planning.

''Thanks, guys.'' Cotter twisted around to shake each boy's hand to confirm their agreement.

While Cotter stayed in the tractor to finish the last of the planting, Pippa and the boys returned to the house to do the feeding. Though Lexie was thrilled to find the yellow police ribbon tacked across the shed opening, Pippa was annoyed that she couldn't run the calves in to feed as she usually did.

As Vance let Rube out of the barn stall, he said to his mother, ''Rube's knocked some boards off in there.'' And turning to the goat, he held her head in both hands, his face close to hers, and scolded, ''Rube, you've been a bad girl again. It's okay to guard us, but when we put you up, then you should know the people are okay.'' Far from being contrite, Rube rubbed her face against Vance's cheek. She let out a soft baa as if protesting her ignominious confinement.

''Dumb goat doesn't understand what you say,'' Lexie said.

''She does too.''

''Does n—'' Lexie stopped, realizing this was not fit behavior for a Greenlee partner. ''Okay,'' he admitted, ''she's not dumb.'' To further concede his point, he too rubbed Rube's head, fingering the short curly wool between her smooth horns.

Pippa smiled. They were learning. ''After you feed her, Vance, put her out in the hog lot and shut the gate.''

''Aw, Mom, she won't like it.''

''She'll get lonely out there,'' Lexie said.

''It's her own fault. I can't have her tearing up the place. Look at the trouble she's caused already, ruining Cotter's pants, digging up bones that bring the sheriff out here, and now I'll have to repair the stall.''

First one thing and then another. No matter how much a pet Rube was, Pippa wasn't going to let an animal disrupt her plans or cause extra trouble. She steeled herself against Rube's dignified bearing. Without looking into the goat's bright eyes, she said, ''That's it. To the hog lot with her until she gets used to Cotter being around.''

Chapter Six

After so much excitement, the next two weeks passed uneventfully—almost dull in comparison. Cotter moved into the efficiency apartment above the machinery barn and quickly became a familiar figure on the farm. Whenever Pippa needed him, he helped her with the livestock and with maintenance work on the farm; the rest of the time he spent tramping through the pastures, drawing and photographing plants. Rube remained banished to the hog lot, pacing the fence whenever Cotter came near. The wheat sprouted nicely, soon carpeting the fields with fresh luminescent green.

The excitement in the county over the discovery of the body soon died down. Though people were intrigued with the headlines about finding a body on the Greenlee farm, no one was more than mildly curious about who the dead man was, nor did anyone else think about a possible connection to the unknown grave. The long article in the paper quoting the historical society's spokesman reported that the body was probably that

of an outlaw because for years after the Civil War bands
of famous and not-so-famous outlaws operated in and
around the county. The time of this murder was in the
era of Jesse and Frank James and the Younger brothers.

"People were killed by outlaws who robbed them
of their money or ran off their cattle," the historian
was quoted. "Many times ruthless men needed no motive, but just killed, continuing the tactics of the bushwhackers of the Civil War. Law enforcement was
inadequate to control this element. Sometimes local
people, alone or working as a group of vigilantes, killed
an outlaw. The body discovered on the Greenlee farm,
since it was obviously buried quickly and secretly in
the barn where the animals would cover up any evidence of a grave, was probably an outlaw killed by a
local farmer. He wouldn't report it, fearing repercus-
sions from the outlaw's gang, nor, of course, would
the other outlaws."

To justify this position, the article quoted two local
sources of historically documented outlaw activity in
the area during the 1870s. For several days after the
first article appeared, there were additional short no-
tices and letters to the editor about comparable inci-
dents up until the early 1880s when the authorities
finally put a stop to the lawlessness.

The sheriff sent his evidence to the state crime lab-
oratory. The official report confirmed the original di-
agnosis from his own office: sometime in the mid
1870s, a Caucasian man in his upper twenties was
killed by a close-range, twelve-gauge shotgun blast to
the head. The sheriff's official report satisfied everyone. "It is our conclusion," the paper quoted him,
"that the body was that of an outlaw, probably shot

in the act of robbing the house or rustling cattle. It was undoubtedly done in self-defense, the outlaw being shot in a struggle over the gun. Since the killing happened so long ago that it couldn't matter to anyone now, I've closed the case.''

The sheriff was mistaken. The killing *did* matter to the Greenlees and Cotter. No matter how long ago it happened, Pippa didn't want an unsolved murder on her farm that might have involved one of Vance and Lexie's ancestors. Cotter, as well as Pippa, was interested because they believed this man could be Herb, Ivy Lewis's missing lover.

Privately, the sheriff told Pippa and Cotter that the examiner found one other clue in the bones. The femur, or the right thighbone, had a badly healed, oblique fracture. The man probably limped. The buttons and belt buckle he found with the bones were common, though expensive, items of that era. Although they were an aid to help pinpoint the time of the murder and strengthened the theory that he was an outlaw, they gave no clues as to the man's identity.

This further evidence didn't change Cotter and Pippa's theory that the man was Herb Smith. There were too many coincidences, but they needed more information. Perhaps they would never find out.

One afternoon Pippa and Cotter were putting up the horses after they finished moving the cattle into another section of the pasture. There was still grass in this meadow that might last two or three more weeks. Then she would begin feeding hay to the cattle. In a few days, she planned to put out one of the big round bales to supplement the late grasses. Observing how quickly the cattle cleaned it up would let her know when she needed to start feeding in earnest.

Cotter removed the saddles and brushed the horses. The mare trotted around the paddock, kicking playfully at the gelding.

"That about does it for today," Pippa said, pausing to admire the view of her farm. The gently rolling acres under the bright October sun were cast in shades of green, tan, and brown. To the east the trees of the pastures hid that border of her land, but to the south, nothing stopped her gaze until it reached the hedges of Osage orange trees. This row of thorny trees, planted on section lines and farm borders over a hundred years ago, was now an interlocking, living fence that cattle could not penetrate. As always, Pippa was comforted by the peaceful and well-cared-for open spaces of cropland and hay fields.

As she enjoyed the view, she recalled the small tract in the extreme southeast corner that was hidden from her sight by the swell of the land. Because of a draw running across that corner and the wetness of the ground around it, no one had ever farmed that small parcel of land. The Greenlee men had kept out the weed trees and occasionally burned it off, so that there remained some native grasses and forbs. She wondered why she hadn't thought to tell Cotter of this plot before. She looked at her watch. Plenty of time.

"Say, Cotter, there's a piece of land I want to show you. I sort of forgot about it, because it's small, maybe five acres. You might find some plants there that aren't in the pastures." When Cotter showed interest, she added, "Get your camera equipment and I'll drive you there."

They left the pickup in the adjoining hay field. With his Nikons hanging over his shoulders from their wide straps, Cotter grabbed Pippa's hand and hurried to cross the wet draw. Laughing, they jumped the trickle of water, but landed in some mire.

Unmindful of his muddy boots, Cotter's face was glowing. The area along the draw was a mass of color. Pulling Pippa after him, he stepped from flower to flower, telling her their names and some information about each. There was a patch of tall sunflowers waving in the wind and a thicket of shorter goldenrod. The purple heads of coneflowers stood erect while the long magenta florets drooped below. Bordering the draw he found some New England asters, their lavender blossoms in clusters reaching his shoulders. Nearby were some of the shorter, many-branched white heath asters.

Cotter hugged Pippa quickly before unsnapping his camera case. "Perfect," he said.

When Cotter began taking pictures, Pippa found a stump to sit on. She, like Cotter, was enthralled with the natural beauty of this small corner of prairie. She joined in his enthusiasm. But even more than admiring the flowers, she enjoyed watching Cotter. He was a combination of childish enthusiasm and curiosity with professional expertise and inquiry. He almost danced among the flowers, his eyes eager and alive, while at the same time his beard and stylishly shaped longish hair indicated a serious, scholarly person.

Pippa admired his ease in handling his equipment and his talent in selecting just the right artistic angle to take the shot. His concentration impressed her. Once he started working, he seemed to be in a world apart. Carefully, so as not to step on a flower, he circled individual plants, sighting them from all sides before taking any pictures.

As he moved from one flower to another, he glanced at her as if to see if she was still there and if she was noticing. He'd nod, raise his hand, or make some other motion to acknowledge her presence, but he didn't say anything. Pippa smiled back, happy that she thought of mentioning this plot.

He worked his way down the draw toward the south hedge line. To keep him in view, Pippa followed behind him. Suddenly he stopped and tensed up. From his frozen posture, Pippa's first thought was that he saw a snake. She likewise stopped, searching the ground for the snake. Where he was staring, all she saw was a big clump of pale-blue asters.

"Outstanding!" he said.

Since it wasn't a snake, Pippa moved beside him to see.

"Pippa, do you know what this plant is?" Then without giving her time to answer he said, "It's a rare aster—a natural hybrid. I've only seen it once before."

He knelt down on one knee to touch one cluster of blooms. He lovingly cupped one of the dime-size flowerets in his fingers, his thumb caressing the yellow center and then running over the many light-blue florets radiating from it in all directions.

"This is a rare find." With his free hand, he reached out for Pippa's, clenched his fingers around her hand, just as quickly let go, and then stepped back to survey the area. He saw several more asters along the draw and, almost hidden by the tall seed heads of prairie switchgrass, spied a few scattered flowers extending back toward the hedge.

"I didn't know hybrid plants occurred naturally," Pippa said. She wondered if his quick touch was gratitude for her showing him this patch of ground or for affection for her. Maybe both? She hoped so. His touch thrilled her.

"Oh, yes. That's why we have so many different varieties of each species." He stepped over to another cluster. "This hybrid is a cross of the white heath aster over there, and the New England aster—that lavender aster just beyond it. This is a perfect habitat for hybridization to occur."

Then without saying more, he started photographing the hybrid aster, taking more time and pains than with any of the other blossoms. When he finished, he took Pippa's hand to walk over the entire triangular plot. It didn't take them long to cover it. They didn't find any different species than they'd already seen. Nearer to the hedge, the vegetation was lighter and tended toward the more drought-resistant plants like dock and mullein. The hedge roots sapped the ground of moisture for several rods into the field.

After covering the tract, they rested on a log. From their location they could see beyond the terraced fields to the farm buildings and on behind them to the bare cottonwood trees by the unknown grave. From this slightly higher ground, they could look into the pasture where the cattle were grazing on their new grass. The mid-afternoon sun on the ponds was reflected in irregular glints as the wind disturbed the water's surface.

"I love it here," Cotter said. "It's like my part of Texas, only greener, richer. Wide-open spaces, but not depressing in their expanse."

"I like it too, though I've always lived in this

county—this township, to be exact.'' Pippa reached up to pick a sunflower blossom. Unconsciously she began pulling off the yellow petals. ''I've seen some whole fields that were planted to sunflowers. Late in the fall the seeds were harvested by combines.''

''I have too. Out in Kansas there are lots of fields. I was there once in October when they were in full bloom. A spectacular sight!''

''Yeah. Rows and rows of yellow blossoms. The cultivated ones I saw weren't tall like these here, but about three feet high. All of the heads were facing east. It was like thousands and thousands of little faces all staring at me. Each one seemed to be saying, 'Pippa, see how beautiful I am? Plant me. Plant me.' ''

Cotter laughed. ''I can see where Lexie gets his imagination from.''

She stopped pulling off the petals and pointed to the hay field where her pickup truck was parked. ''The hay yield on that field this year was poor. The field needs reseeding. So I've been thinking about putting it in sunflowers next spring. What do you think?''

He glanced over the field and then back to Pippa's hands that were busy again pulling the petals from her sunflower blossom. ''I think I've lost count,'' he said, grinning.

She looked at him, her eyebrows contracted, as she tried to figure out what he was talking about.

''Yeah,'' Cotter explained. ''With all your inter-ruptions about planting fields of sunflowers, I've lost count of your petals on that sunflower head.''

Pippa held poised in mid-air a thin yellow petal. Cotter stroked his beard, his eyes mischievous. ''Is it, 'He loves me,' or 'He loves me not?' '' he teased, and jumped across the draw toward the hay field, but not before Pippa hit him playfully across his arm.

She caught up with him and held to his arm as they walked. "Now seriously, what do you think about planting sunflowers?"

"I think it's a good idea. You have all the equipment—planter, combine. That field should be ideal. Look at all the wild sunflowers all around it."

"I don't think I'll put the whole field in to start with, maybe just twenty acres. To see how it does."

Cotter nodded his approval and rested his hand on hers, which was on his arm. "Not only do I like this country, I like this farm. You've got a good thing here."

"I know."

"Pretty sure of yourself, aren't you?" he teased.

"Yes, most of the time." No, she really wasn't, but she was playing the game. Her face showed her amusement.

Cotter stopped and looked directly at her. "You're pretty terrific too," he said.

"I know." Pippa laughed and sprinted ahead of him to the pickup.

Burdened down with his camera equipment, Cotter couldn't catch up to her. When he reached the truck, Pippa was already in the driver's seat with the engine running.

"Hurry up, slowpoke," she said. "I see the school bus on the highway."

Chapter Seven

One Saturday while Cotter was away on a hurried trip back to Texas to get his darkroom equipment and more of his belongings, the boys and Pippa decided to do some historical research at home to find out more about the Greenlee family in the 1870s. Keeping them company was Freewill. With his tail neatly wrapped around his sleek body, he was perched on the bed where he could oversee the operation. Pippa started looking through the family papers that were stashed away in dresser drawers in the guest room. Since the family had lived on the land since the 1830s, there were many papers, documents, and photographs saved over the years and carefully stored in the drawer.

Someone, in a shaky but legible hand, had written out a rather complete genealogy and family history from Colonial times in Virginia up to 1953. By studying the birth and death dates, Pippa figured that in the mid-1870s Isaac Greenlee owned the home place. She already knew that her house was built by Doug's father in 1954. The old house, located about a city block east of the "new" house, had been turned into a hog shed, but was in such disreputable state that on Pippa's urging, it was torn down soon after she moved to the farm after her marriage. At the time of the murder, the Greenlees were living in the old house, farther away from the unknown grave than her present house.

Looking at Isaac's dates, she figured he was forty-seven in 1876, the time of the murder at the unknown grave. A widower at the time, he had three married daughters, who probably wouldn't have been at home. He also had two sons—the twins' ancestor, Olin, whose wife was named Opal, and a younger son, Seth, who was fifteen at the time. Olin and Seth were the next co-owners of the farm, and then down in a line to Doug and her. There was no record of Seth marrying, though he stayed on the farm until his death in 1954. After his death, the farm came to Doug's father and on his death to Doug. Now it belonged to Pippa.

"If someone on the farm killed our guy in the barn, or the unknown woman, then it must have been old Isaac, or his sons Olin or Seth," Lexie said, stretched out on the bed on his stomach listening attentively to every word his mother read. Freewill was lounging beside him.

"Don't forget Olin's wife, Opal," Pippa said.

Lexie screwed up his face in doubt that a woman could have killed a man.

"But," Pippa said, "just because they were the ones who were living here at the time, that doesn't mean that any of them had anything to do with it."

"Yeah, but some of them must have known something or seen something." Lexie rubbed Freewill under his chin. The cat purred loudly.

"You would think so. People don't get buried in your barn without you suspecting something."

"Or doing it themselves," Lexie said.

"Okay, then, let's find out all we can about those four people."

Vance was getting bored with this. He wanted to be outside on the beautiful November Saturday instead of poring over yellowed and stuffy-smelling papers of ancient history. "Do I have to?" he asked.

"No, of course not, Vance," Pippa said. "Go on and play."

"I'll keep looking," Lexie said.

That suited Pippa. Though wanting to find out about the murder, she knew a dozen jobs she should be doing. After all, these murders happened over a hundred years ago. A few more days' delay wouldn't matter. She and Vance left Lexie sitting cross-legged on the floor in front of an open bureau drawer, happily lifting out packages of papers tied with string or rag strips and carefully laying them in piles around him. Still on the bed, Freewill curled up, ready to take a nap.

As she gathered up hammer, staples, a roll of wire, and wire cutters to repair the hog lot fence where Rube had damaged a section, Pippa was surprised at her good mood. Even her anger toward the pesky goat that was causing unnecessary problems didn't depress her as it used to do. In her old age, Rube was becoming more trouble than she was worth. But Pippa realized that on a scale of ten, the annoyance rated a two at most—not serious enough to haul Rube off to the stockyards. She admitted that since Cotter's arrival, the thought had crossed her mind, but she discarded it because the boys were so fond of Rube. So was she.

The past few months when she had to do nuisance tasks like repairing this fence, she would become depressed, feel sorry for herself, and ask why she had to do it. She often wondered if there was any end to the demands on her. But today, with Rainy beside her, quivering in anticipation of an outing in the pasture, she gathered up her tools in a happy mood, even looking forward to being outside in the brisk morning. Vance was right. This beat being closed up in the house poring over ancient documents.

Rube met her at the hog lot gate, her wool a whitish blob against the scarlet leaves of the sumac along the fence. The goat's whole demeanor denoted depression. Her head was hanging low, clods of dirt hanging from her usually clean coat.

"Baa-a-a," Rube pleaded, her eyes watching Pippa open the gate. Pippa relented and held the gate open for her to return to the barnyard. No reason to keep her penned with the hogs while Cotter was gone. Besides, Cotter was the interloper, Rube the longtime resident. Well, from now on it would have to be Cotter's problem. He was a resourceful man. It was up to him to keep out of Rube's way.

"Okay, Rube, ol' girl," she said, fondling the goat's head and pulling out some burrs caught behind a long silky ear. "You win. You can stay in the barnyard."

Rube lifted her head and stepped in her stately and dignified manner to the barn, where Vance met her. He hugged her, then running into the barn, returned with a curry comb and brush. Pippa knew that he would not stop until Rube's coat hung silky and rippling, almost touching the ground.

Thinking of Cotter put another smile on Pippa's face.

She already missed him, though he'd been away only a few days—four to be exact. He had become so much a part of the farm that it seemed like she'd known him much longer than two weeks. Their arrangement was working out well. Though he hadn't been on a farm since he was a kid, he remembered what to do. With very little coaching, he could do whatever she needed, just as he took over the tractor and wheat drill that first day. Then a few days ago when he asked if he could stay until the end of the year, Pippa felt as if she should grasp something to keep from floating away. Such a weight was lifted from her that gravity couldn't hold her down.

She began humming as she mended the hole in the woven wire where Rube had forced her head through and then couldn't pull her head back out. Her horns trapped her there until Vance had to cut the wire to free her. Pippa stapled the loose wire firmly to the post, realizing how badly Rube had wanted out to get caught that way. The goat learned years ago how to prevent the wire from trapping her. She turned her head slightly to one side and pointed her nose up so that her horns touched her neck. In that position, she could pull her head back through the meshes of the wire without her horns trapping her head. None of the brush goats in the big pastures ever learned that. Pippa's solution was to use the smallest mesh woven wire she could get so the goats couldn't poke their heads through in the first place.

After fixing the one bad spot, she walked the fence to check for any other breaks. It was more serious for the hogs to get out than for Rube. The goat simply came to the house, never straying. On the other hand, the hogs, especially the little pigs, would squeeze through or crawl under any weak place in the fence. Once free they would scamper off and just keep running. Until she and Doug built this fence five years ago, the hogs had to be chased all over the neighborhood. The little pigs still managed to get out occasionally if she didn't keep a close watch over the fence. Busy with the corn and soybean harvest, she hadn't inspected the wire for a few weeks.

She hiked along the fencerow admiring the goldenrod and wild blue asters across the fence along the shoulder of the country road. Rainy was covering the lot, nose to the ground, running back and forth in front of her. Suddenly he was on point, immobile as a statue.

"Whatcha got there, boy?" Pippa walked cautiously in front of his point. About a dozen quail exploded into the air. Pippa knelt beside the dog and hugged him. "Good boy." They watched the birds fly low over the fence and land in the rough land across the road. Pippa had to hold him to keep him from following. "Not today, boy." She was happy to know that Rainy hadn't forgotten his training.

When she reached the leafless persimmon tree loaded with ripe fruit, she spotted the matted-down grass and the telltale tunnel-like hole burrowed under the fence where the little pigs had pushed up the bottom wire. They were probably after the persimmons fallen on the other side of the fence.

"Oh, darn," she said to Rainy, her pleasant mood ruined. She quickly counted the sows. They were all accounted for, stretched out contentedly on the ground, their little pigs suckling greedily. One big sow was lying on a grassy knoll, but her ever-present pigs were not with her.

"Vance!" Pippa yelled, dropping her tools and climbing over the fence to the road. "Samantha's pigs are out. Looks like they've headed to the railroad." She didn't look back to see if he was coming, but ran across the road. For some reason the railroad seemed to be a magnet for the pigs. She could nearly always find them there if they got out along the road fence.

On the other side of the road from the hog lot, the railroad tracks were across a neck of rough land where the quail landed. This woody area, enclosed by fields and open pastures on both sides, was the result of the railroad tracks changing direction. Directly in front of the Greenlee house, where the unknown grave was, the tracks began to veer slightly northeast toward town, leaving this widening V-shaped, uncultivated space between them and the road which followed the section line straight east.

After yelling into the house for Lexie to come help, Vance ran across the road to the tracks, then ran up them toward his mother to head off the pigs if they came his way. They met without finding them.

Expecting his mother to blame Rube again for breaking still another hole in the woven wire of the fence, Vance pleaded, "Rube doesn't know she's causing trouble. She only wants to get to the house."

Panting, Pippa was leaning over to ease the pain in her side from running. She held up her hand and shook her head to give time to catch her breath. "It wasn't Rube. The pigs dug under the fence by that big persimmon tree where the ground is soft."

"There they are!" Vance shouted, pointing farther

up the tracks where the pigs were running east away from them as fast as they could. Pippa and Vance had chased and corralled hogs enough to know what to do without instructions. They had to get ahead of the pigs.

Vance rolled under the north fence that separated the railroad right-of-way from their neighbor's wheat field. With Rainy following, Pippa ran wide into the trees and brush in the rough land on the south, startling the quail that flew back across the road. Several rods back on either side, they each ran parallel to the tracks to get around the pigs and stop their headlong flight. Once they got the pigs headed back down the tracks toward home, they hoped that Lexie would be there by the unknown grave to block them and head them across the road and into the lot. Though Rainy kept them company, he continued his scenting for birds and was no help. He was not a stock dog.

The thirteen Hampshire pigs were squealing and grunting with delight at their freedom. One adventurous one would dash off in one direction, the others following, until another would scent something interesting someplace else. They were scurrying over the rails, their little hooves clattering on the iron and thudding against the slate-colored wooden ties. In spite of her annoyance, Pippa admired the playful youngsters. The white stripes circling their bodies around their front legs and shoulders gleamed brightly in the sunlight against their black, round bodies.

Yelling and waving her arms, Pippa managed to group the pigs together between the iron rails and head them back toward home. Finally tired from their adventure, they moved much more slowly now. Vance had grabbed a stick and was tapping errant pigs on their noses when they tried to break away. With so-prano squeals, they would rejoin their littermates.

"Did Lexie hear you?" Pippa asked.

"I don't know."

They didn't see Lexie by the unknown grave where he should be blocking the tracks to turn the pigs.

"Want me to get ahead of them?" Vance asked.

"Yes, unless we want to drive them all the way to the highway crossing. But swing out wide. Don't scare them into bolting again."

Just as Vance reached the road to run around the pigs, Pippa heard the muted whistle of a train engine pulling up the long grade into Ellis. The possibility of a train coming hadn't worried her, because in the past few months the train traffic had almost stopped. She hadn't heard a train for a couple of weeks.

"Vance!" she screamed. "The train! No time to drive them up to the crossing at the grave. Gotta get them off. Now!" At the first sound of the train, Rainy hightailed it home.

But Pippa wasn't too concerned. She had time. The train was still a couple of miles away, and would travel slowly up the grade. Alone, without Vance's help, she couldn't drive the pigs off the tracks. They were deaf to any threats, too frightened by the ominous rumbling in the rails on either side to jump over them. Squealing with fright, and blocked behind by Pippa, they raced straight toward the approaching engine. When Vance showed up again in the weeds several yards to her left, she yelled, "Stay back! Keep back!"

"Mom!" he cried. "Mommy, get off of there." He was running parallel to her, crying. "Leave the stupid pigs."

Pippa made one more effort to turn the pigs. Based on years of experience in listening to the train sounds, without looking up she knew from the loudness of the whistle that the train was already at Ellis and gathering speed on the long level stretch. Less than a mile away! And apparently a short train because it was approaching faster than usual. Waving her arms wildly and shrieking at the pigs, she tore back and forth without turning a single one.

"Mommy!" screamed Vance.

Above the roar of the engine which had now passed beyond the highway crossing less than half a mile away, she heard just ahead of her a deep, "Hee-ya! Hee-ya!"

Suddenly two pigs jumped over the south rail. "Hee-ya! Hee-ya!" came closer still the same deep yell. Then the rest of the litter leaped over the rail and scrambled down the cleared embankment into the brush along the roadside.

Pippa recognized Cotter tearing toward her on the graveled shoulder beside the rails. Right behind the last little pig, Pippa and Cotter slid down the embankment and rolled under the fence just as the locomotive thundered by, its whistle blaring angrily and continuously. The engineer thrust his worried face out his side window and shook his head at them. Cotter waved back.

The danger was over. As fast as their little legs could take them, the pigs, noisily pushing and shoving one another to be first, crawled back under the wire to big Samantha who was pacing the fence and squealing her distress. The last freight car rumbled past. Pippa and Cotter, weak and panting, stood in the middle of the road. Almost instantaneously they hugged each other, laughing and crying together in relief. Vance, who had watched the rescue farther up the road by the grave, ran to them.

"Mommy, you scared me!" Vance was crying. Pippa and Cotter both included him in their hug.

"Don't you ever do such a fool thing again," Cotter scolded Pippa. Though his voice was stern, his yearning eyes holding Pippa's contradicted his angry tone.

"For a moment there, I thought. . . . " He glanced from her to the spot where she left the tracks behind the pigs. Then looking back to Pippa and Vance he said gently, "I knew then how important you've become to me."

Still breathless and shaking from her narrow escape, Pippa put an arm around Vance without removing Cotter's arm encircling her waist. His closeness seemed the normal response after such an experience.

"Mom, you okay?" Vance asked, struggling in her tight embrace and puzzled at her continued silence and unusual behavior.

She smiled at the boy and let go of him. "Yes, sweetie, I'm fine." Since Cotter was expecting some response also, she met his steady gaze.

"Where'd you come from?" she heard herself asking, though she intended to say something about how important he had become to them. "I thought you were still in Texas."

"Drove all night. Good thing too. Couldn't wait to get back to see you guys." He ruffled Vance's hair affectionately.

They watched the train disappear toward town, though for several minutes they continued to hear it whistle every mile at country road crossings. The piglets were already forgetting their narrow escape. Each was actively attacking one of Samantha's teats.

With his arms still around Pippa and Vance, Cotter started leading them slowly toward the house.

"Seems like I got here just in time," he said. "And I've got some more information about our two murder victims." He cocked his head to indicate the unknown grave, and then with a stronger movement of his head, and a know-it-all grin that wiggled his beard, he nodded in the opposite direction toward the barn.

Not to be upstaged, Vance said, "We've got some stuff to tell you too."

"Yes," Pippa said. "We've learned some things that might help us."

"Tell us what you found out," Vance begged Cotter.

"Let's at least get to the house." Suddenly he looked around the lawn. "Where's Lexie?"

"In the house still looking through some old records about the Greenlees who lived here in 1876," Pippa said. "He may have found out some more facts."

"Good," Cotter said. Without removing his right arm from Pippa's waist, and with Vance hanging on to his left hand, he steered them back to the house.

Rainy crawled out from the security of the porch and trotted happily behind them. His tongue, dripping saliva as usual, hung down from his grinning mouth, and his tail wagged as if he were the one that saved the pigs.

Chapter Eight

They found Lexie still in the guest room engrossed in reading from a long, narrow ledger book, unaware of the recent drama outside the window. Scattered on the floor were piles of old books and papers, but he was lying comfortably on his stomach, chest and head propped up by pillows in the middle of the double bed. The book lay open in front of him on the off-white bedspread. Freewill was stretched out on the top edge of the uppermost pillow just beside Lexie's blond head. The cat's striped tail lent a splash of reddish color to the boy's gray sweatshirt as it flicked back and forth across his shoulder.

When Lexie saw the three of them standing in the door, he didn't express surprise at seeing Cotter, but jumped up, upsetting Freewill who dashed out of the room. "Hey, you guys, I found something!" He held the tattered book above his head to prevent Vance from grabbing it.

"I don't care about any old book," Vance said. "Mom almost got run over by the train."

"Yeah, and UFOs just landed in the front lawn," Lexie said.

Ignoring their squabble, Pippa asked, "What did you find, Lexie? Cotter just got back and he said he has some news also."

"I found a diary," he announced proudly, his brown eyes shining with delight. He held the book up for them to see. "It's by Opal Greenlee!"

"Looks like an old account book to me," Vance said unimpressed.

"It is. At first I didn't pay any attention to it, but then I dropped it and saw that there was lots of writing on the pages. See?" He held it up for them to see the fine writing done with black ink.

Pippa explained to Cotter, "Opal Greenlee was the wife of Olin Greenlee. They, Olin's brother Seth, and father Isaac were the ones living here at the time of the murder."

Excited, Cotter stepped to Lexie. "Does it say anything about the murder?" He reached for the book, but Lexie pulled it back, holding it possessively against his chest. Without trying further to get the book or take the spotlight from him, Cotter said, "Tell us what you found out." He turned to Pippa, "Then I'll tell my news."

Pippa nodded for Lexie to begin.

"Well, this Opal, she wrote stuff in the blank spaces and in the back where there wasn't any figures. Most of it was about what she cooked for dinner, about planting a garden, and junk like that. But here's the good part." He made a dramatic pause for them all to appreciate the importance of what he was about to say. Then he read the date, "May 12, 1876." He paused, looking at Cotter and his mother to be sure they realized the significance of that date—the same day that Ivy Lewis wrote her note before she ran away. When they all understood that, he began reading from the old ledger book.

> *"Olin, Father Greenlee, and I are going to Jefferson City tomorrow on the Katy Flyer. I'm excited. Father Greenlee is going back to a short, special committee meeting of the legislature, and he asked Olin and me to join him. Imagine that! Father Greenlee says that Seth is old enough to mind the farm for the few days we'll be gone. Seth is proud his father is giving him this responsibility."*

Now that Lexie had told what he found, he leaned back, smug in his ability as a detective and satisfied with the reaction from his mother and Cotter. Even Vance was impressed.

"So you were right about who lived here at the time." Cotter said.

Pippa nodded happily. "Yes, and this tells us that young Seth was the only one at home for the next few days when the murder probably happened."

"How old was Seth then?" Cotter asked.

"Sixteen. Is there anything else, Lexie?" Pippa urged him. She was anxious to take the diary herself, but allowed Lexie to have his say.

"Naw. Nothing interesting as far as I've got. She goes on telling about what she's going to wear in Jefferson City," Lexie said, turning the page. "Just stupid junk like that and about the trip."

"And when she got back home?" Cotter asked. "Surely she mentioned the body?"

"I haven't read that far."

"May I see it?" Cotter asked.

Lexie was willing to give it up now that he'd added his clue to the mystery.

They returned to the kitchen where Pippa started fixing a lunch. She asked Cotter to stay, though he hadn't eaten with them since that first night when the boys fixed the sandwiches.

"Here it is," Cotter said excitedly. "This one is dated May 18, after they got back from Jefferson City. Listen to this!"

> *"Nothing ever happens in Ellis, people say, but something did today. Father Greenlee was out hunting the hogs that keep getting out of the lot. He headed straight for the railroad tracks as we've had some killed there before. And he found a woman! A dead woman. We all went out to see her. We didn't know her. She'd been dead a few days; I could tell and Father Greenlee said so too. Oh, it was awful. I won't describe it or I'll get sick just remembering. Seth did get sick, and probably would have run off if Father Greenlee hadn't sent him to Ellis to wire the law. The woman was real young, surely not yet twenty. She was dressed in fancy clothes, though they were bloody and torn by somebody or some animal—maybe even our hogs. I can hardly stand to think about that. Her clothes were stylish like those I saw some*

*rich women in Jefferson City wearing. The
law came and there was lots of excitement
here for a while. No one knows who she is,
or what happened to the man that was with
her when they got off the train at Ellis. Maude
told me all about it. She was there and saw
them. Maude said the woman was red in the
face as if she'd been crying. And she run up
the tracks toward our place with the man
limping along behind trying to keep up with
her. They buried her right where Father
Greenlee found her. Poor dear.''*

"Limping!" Pippa said. "Then our guy from the
barn was with the unknown woman in the grave."

"Undoubtedly." Cotter's eyes shown brightly. He
scanned the diary for more. "This seems to be all that
Opal wrote about it. The only thing she says is that
she was worried about Seth. She wrote several days
later, 'Seth seems moody and not his usual self. He
mopes around. I quietly do some of his chores for him
so Father Greenlee won't be so hard on him.' That's
all."

"I like that Opal," Pippa said, handing the account
book back to Lexie. "Here, keep this book safe. This
is your great-great—I'll figure out later how many
times—grandmother. There is probably lots of good
stuff in here about the family besides the murder."

Scooping out bowls of soup, she turned to Cotter.
"Now what is your news?"

"I was convinced before that the unknown woman
was Ivy Lewis, and now after reading Opal Greenlee's
diary, I'm quite sure that the man with her, and the

one Vance found in your barn, was her boyfriend, Herb. While I was home in Denison getting my stuff, I visited my aunt to pump her about anything she ever heard about Ivy. She told the same old stuff that I knew and had heard many times, but she added a couple of new facts I never heard or have forgotten.

"First, this Herb guy went by the name of Smith. The family believed that wasn't his real name. One reason the family was so opposed to him was his secretiveness about his background and not revealing his real name. He claimed he was from the West, but he spoke with a Missouri accent. He had lots of money with no explanation as to how he got it."

"Anything else?" Pippa asked when he paused.

"Yes." He looked at each of them to dramatize his next statement. "Herb Smith walked with a slight limp."

"We've solved it," Lexie said happily, clapping his hands together. "That's Ivy Lewis out there and Herb Smith is the guy in the shed." He paused and corrected himself, "*Was* in the shed."

"It certainly seems that way," Cotter said.

Vance was excited that the body he found had a name.

"Then we're sort of related," Lexie said. "That's your relative that was killed and our relative that found her body."

"Well," Cotter said, laughing, "let's just say there is a connection."

"We've solved the murder," Lexie stated again.

"Not so fast," Pippa said. "All we know is the identity of the bodies. We still don't know why Ivy left the train at Ellis and walked up here, why they were arguing, or who killed her, or—''

"Herb killed her," Lexie said, " 'cause she wouldn't wait for him and for being so stupid as to get off the train in Nowheresville.''

"Dummy," Vance said, "people don't kill other people just for getting off at a wrong station, even if it is Nowheresville." Lexie's new name for Ellis intrigued him.

"Unlikely," Cotter agreed, "but let's say, just to speculate a bit here, even if that's what happened, then where did Herb get the shotgun to kill her?"

"And more puzzling yet, who killed him and buried him in our shed?" Pippa shook her head in bewilderment. "We already knew the approximate day when the woman's murder happened. Now we know who she was, and who the guy in the shed was—at least his alias. But we don't have a clue as to why they were killed or how.''

"They were shot. With a twelve-gauge shotgun," Lexie reminded her. "That's how they were killed."

"At least Herb's death was from a twelve-gauge, yes," Pippa said. "Ivy was shot, but we don't know what kind of gun. But how did it happen and why?"

"You mean the motive?" Lexie asked.

"Right. The motive, and how did the events occur that left two dead people at Isaac Greenlee's place?"

While the four of them finished their lunch, none of them could come up with even a logical theory. "We'll probably never find the answer to that," Pippa said.

Cotter agreed. "Not after so much time. If anyone ever knew besides the dead couple, they too are long dead.''

They were all silent for a few minutes. Lexie said, "Maybe aliens in a UFO happened by and—"

"Oh, you and your ol' UFOs." Vance moaned. Lexie stuck his tongue out at him.

With much experience, Pippa knew the best way to avoid another argument from the boys was to get their minds on something else.

"Say, guys, why don't you help Cotter unload his van? He's brought all his darkroom equipment." She looked at Cotter, hoping her suggestion was okay with him.

"Good idea," Cotter said, nodding to Pippa. "I can sure use some muscle."

Immediately the twins were on their feet to help. "I've gotten you each something," Cotter said as he stood up and led the way. On each side of him was a boy begging him to tell them what he'd brought.

"Watch out for Rube," Pippa called after them as the kitchen door slammed shut. "She's in the barn-yard."

"I'll really have to concentrate on making friends with her," Cotter said.

The next morning when Pippa opened the gate to the barnyard, Rube was waiting for her as usual. Pippa rubbed the goat's head, talking to her before she noticed that Cotter was already in the lot feeding the calves. Rainy was following his every step as usual, but. . . . She paused in petting Rube and realized that the goat was ignoring Cotter's presence. She leaned contently against Pippa as if the two of them were alone in the lot.

"You did it!" Pippa called to Cotter. "Rube has accepted you."

"Nothing to it," Cotter called back. His back was to her as he was pouring ground corn from a heavy burlap sack into the feeding troughs. The calves were crowding close to him, anxious to bury their noses in the grain.

"How'd you do it?" By this time she and the goat had reached Cotter. Rube still showed no signs of antagonism.

For an answer, Cotter turned around, removed his hat, and grinned broadly. His smiling face was bare of mustache and beard. His white skin where the hair once covered it made quite a contrast to the rest of his tanned face.

"You shaved off your beard?" Pippa asked, and then laughed at her unnecessary question.

"Yeah. And it did the trick. Something Lexie said gave me the idea. He said that Rube didn't like me because my beard was prettier than Rube's." He stroked his bare chin and looked at Rube, who was quietly standing just behind Pippa. "Nothing I could do before did any good with her. She still hated me. So I made the ultimate sacrifice. I shaved off my beard and mustache. And presto—Rube accepts me. She lets me into her kingdom. See?"

To prove his point he walked toward Rube. The alert goat allowed him to pat her on the head just once before she walked away haughtily. No lowered head in the butting position. No pacing or restlessness. But her manner left no doubts that though she wasn't belligerent anymore, she still considered him beneath her.

Pippa laughed so hard she had to hold on to the side

of the feed trough. She hadn't had such a good laugh since. . . .

"Well," Cotter asked, "how do you like it?" He again stroked his denuded chin.

Composing herself, since Cotter was quite serious, she studied his face. Without the facial hair, his brown eyes were more noticeable. The morning light accented glints of the same auburn color as his hair. His lips were full and soft, turned up slightly at each corner, giving him a jaunty air. She hadn't noticed before that there was a slight gap between his top front teeth. He was very handsome. But she missed the beard.

"How do you like it?" he asked again, becoming uncomfortable under her direct stare, even though he had asked her to look at him.

"Handsome," she answered. "Younger, maybe, but definitely handsome." She realized what a sacrifice he must have made for their sakes, just to appease the pesky goat. His habit of stroking his beard and the care he took to always keep it neatly trimmed showed how much he must have valued it. So did she. "But I think I liked your face better with the beard," she added.

"Me too." He rubbed his hand across his chin again, this time also stroking his bare upper lip with his forefinger. "Gives me a more distinguished look, don't you think?"

"Well, maybe. A different look, certainly."

"But shaving it off is for a good cause. I've overcome the last objection to my being here."

Cotter's grin spread across his face. "Pippa, driving back yesterday I could hardly wait to get here. All the way I kept thinking about you. And the boys and the farm. Even ol' Rube there." They both looked toward the barn where Rube had retired, lying down in her customary pose warming herself in the early-morning sun. Freewill was climbing over her back, searching out the most comfortable place to settle in her heavy woolen coat.

Cotter's face was serious. "Then when I turned off the highway onto your road, I felt like I was coming home. I really knew how much you meant when I saw you out on the tracks with the train locomotive bearing down on you. In the few seconds it took us to get those pigs off the tracks I learned something about myself."

He paused for a few minutes. Pippa didn't say anything. They both had stepped back from the trough away from the calves. Only faintly could she hear the soft sounds of the calves munching and scraping the wooden bottom of the trough. She was trying to sort out her emotions. Not knowing what to do or say, and afraid her eyes would give away feelings she herself couldn't define, she stooped to pet Rainy.

Cotter looked steadily at Pippa. "I probably shouldn't ask. I know I should give you more time, but I'd very much like to kiss you."

His words caught her off guard, even though she was expecting something more intimate than their usual exchange. Cotter had become a valuable helper, a trusted friend. But more serious than that? She didn't think she could ever be interested in another man. Why, the first time she ever saw him she was grieving for her dead husband.

She unconsciously took a step backward and looked at him. His unwavering eyes forced hers to lock with his. There was no hurt in his when she retreated, only disappointment.

"I'm sorry. I spoke out of place. Forget I even said it." Cotter put his hat back on and started toward the barn with the empty feed sack.

"I'd like you to kiss me," Pippa heard herself saying, though she didn't know where the words came from.

Dropping the sack, Cotter put both arms around her gently and, holding her to him, kissed her gently on the lips. He raised his head to look at her and said before letting her go, "Thanks, Pippa. You're a great person." He gave her a playful squeeze. "I've been wanting to do that ever since I first saw you."

He picked up the sack and disappeared into the barn, whistling.

Standing alone in the middle of the barnyard, Pippa couldn't sort out her sensations. The strength of his arms around her, the tender pressure on her lips, his smooth, cool face against hers—it had been so long since she'd felt the elation, the pleasure, the security of a man's arms about her.

Also guilt. Definitely there was guilt. How could she feel so happy with someone else? Not two years since Doug's death! She remembered the familiar closeness they used to have. But her memory of that love was not in any way lessened by this different attraction. Pippa turned and slowly walked back to the house. What would Doug have thought about Cotter? As she often did, she searched her mind to ascertain his reaction.

"You cannot grieve always. You should be happy," she knew he would have said. "People are not meant to live and work alone."

She still felt the tingling that had surged through her

with Cotter's kiss. Her face lit up with a happy smile as she stepped onto the patio and opened the kitchen door to start fixing breakfast.

"Lexie, Vance! Hey, you guys, time to get up. We've got a great day ahead of us."

Chapter Nine

Rainy froze on point as they walked the east fence line of the hog lot. The boys and Cotter stopped in their tracks while Pippa edged slowly forward. While she stepped closer to the hidden birds, Cotter prepared to shoot. The pointer froze when he got the scent, one forefoot raised, his nose, body, and tail forming a straight line to a spot in the undergrowth by the fence.

Pippa shoved her foot into the dried weeds to flush the covey of quail. Suddenly a dozen birds flew up in front of her and headed toward the boys and Cotter. They flew swiftly, filling the air with the whirl of wings.

Cotter got two shots before Lexie found one quail in his viewfinder. By then it was too far away, but he took a picture anyway. Vance didn't even get his camera focused, he was so interested in watching the birds.

"Watch where the birds land," Cotter said softly.

Pippa noted one quail that disappeared in the dead grass at the edge of the hog lot and another that flew into the trees across the fence in the pasture.

112

Rainy looked at his people with his head cocked. He'd done his part of the job, found the quail. Now he was ready to retrieve the dead birds, but there were no shots. No dead birds.

Cotter patted his head. "Good boy, Rainy. Good boy." Then he said to the boys, "He's puzzled because he was expecting to fetch the dead birds. He doesn't understand our kind of hunting."

The Sunday afternoon after Cotter returned from Texas, he took them quail hunting. His gift to each of the boys was a Pentax camera with a zoom lens from his collection—a better and more advanced one than the simple automatic cameras they knew how to use. He had spent time the previous afternoon teaching them how to focus and how to use the built-in light meters.

Since photographing plants was not interesting to the active boys, Pippa suggested they take Rainy quail hunting to photograph him in action. No one expected the boys to get good pictures of the birds, but Cotter was expecting to get some excellent shots as the light was just right.

Pippa pointed to the spots where the two birds landed. Vance saw another and Cotter watched two light. Cotter called Rainy and began searching for the scattered birds. The pointer loped ahead of the group, circling back and forth to cover more ground. Not finding a bird at one place, he'd cross over to another. While Rainy searched, Cotter was constantly at alert. His eyes missed nothing within view. Occasionally he stooped to take a picture of something on the ground, or swung around to catch the rapt expression on Vance's face. Yet he was ready the second Rainy pointed.

Rainy finally scented a quail. Alarmed this time, it flew up right in front of him. Cotter snapped a picture. As he advanced the film, his broad grin spread across his face. Neither boy had time to shoot. Even if Pippa had held a camera, she wouldn't have taken a picture either, for she was too busy watching Cotter.

His khaki vest was filled with rolls of film, extra lenses and filters, and his ever-present, small spiral notebook into which he frequently jotted notes. He handled his equipment effortlessly, switching between the two cameras hanging around his neck, changing lenses, adding filters, and reloading. Even while his hands were doing these things, his eyes were scanning the scene to find his next shot. He paused to give the twins some suggestions, and he frequently turned his face toward Pippa. The corners of his mouth turned up in a perky grin.

When the group failed to find any more of the scattered covey, they crossed the fence into the big pasture. Their course was far from straight, circling about behind Rainy, though the pointer ran five miles to their one. The four of them kept about ten yards apart to cover more ground, walking through blackberry briars, over fallen tree trunks, and through the tall bluestem grasses that completely hid the boys in places where the cattle hadn't grazed. Every time they circled out of the wooded areas to the wider-open spaces, Pippa hoped they might pick easier walking. But they only crossed over the level tracts where the cattle had eaten down the grass. Rainy quickly covered the ground and started hunting in the rougher area where most of the quail were hiding.

They crisscrossed the pastures for more than an hour

before Rainy found another covey. They had plenty of time to admire the Angus herd that was resting by one of the ponds. The cattle, raising their heads curiously when the people intruded, watched them as long as they were in sight, but continued chewing their cuds. The brown brush goats, however, bounded away when Rainy came close. With graceful leaps, they followed the big billy across the ditches of the creek and disappeared.

With Rainy on point again, Cotter put up his hand to warn everyone to stand very still. This time the boys had time to get ready.

Before Pippa stepped in to flush the covey, Cotter said, "This is perfect. Hold on a minute, Pippa."

He instructed the boys where to stand. Speaking softly to prevent disturbing the birds, he said, "Now sight your cameras on that pecan tree over there." He pointed to the lone tree about fifteen yards away. "About halfway up. See that dead limb?" When the boys nodded as they looked at it through their cameras, he said, "Focus on it. Now, keep your camera to your eye and point it over here where Rainy tells us the quail are. No, Lexie, don't change your focus. Watch the action through the lens. As soon as the birds fly out of the grass, take a picture. See, you've already got the focus set, 'cause they will fly away from us toward that pecan tree." Hardly breathing in their eagerness, the boys waited, poised just as Cotter suggested.

He turned toward Pippa. "This is pretty difficult photography for beginners, but they're doing well."

"Yes, they are." Now that the boys and Cotter were ready, Pippa flushed out the covey.

This time only a single bird flew out. Pippa then stepped closer to the tall clump of grass that hid the covey to flush out the others. Eight or ten more followed the first bird toward the pecan tree and into the grove of cottonwood trees behind it, disappearing without landing.

"I got 'em!" Vance shouted. "I saw them through the lens and took a picture."

"Me too!" Lexie said. "Just as they flew by the tree. And they were in focus!" *This action photography is okay,* he thought.

From the pleased expression on Cotter's face, Pippa knew that he was also successful.

"Can we go develop these now, Cotter?" Lexie asked.

"Sure," Cotter said. "I expect you've had enough for today."

For the last half hour Lexie had been complaining—too much boring time between shots. Now that he had his picture, he was ready to go in. He'd had enough tramping through mud and dead weeds and getting his jeans and jacket snagged by briars and covered with the sticky beggar's-lice. Vance was also ready to go in, although he enjoyed being outside with his mother and Cotter.

After jotting down a few notes, Cotter put the lens cover on one of his Nikons and snapped it in its case, though he kept the other camera handy in case he saw a good subject to photograph. With his free hand he took hold of Pippa's as they headed back toward the house. The boys bounded on either side of them, sometimes ahead and sometimes behind. Rainy, realizing the hunt was over, and tired from his unaccustomed exercise, trotted happily beside Vance.

"You're a good pointer, Rainy," Vance said, stroking him and fondling his ears. "Daddy trained him good, didn't he, Mom?"

Without a trace of the usual sadness when the boys mentioned their father, Pippa smiled and said, "Yes, he did, and Rainy hasn't forgotten a thing."

"He's a fine dog," Cotter agreed. He winked at Pippa and said to the boys, "But I had a pointer once that'd beat Rainy here all to pieces."

Vance didn't like the idea that any dog could be better than his.

Cotter continued, "This dog of mine was sharp as a tack. When I carried a shotgun she wouldn't do anything but set quail. If I had my rifle, she'd tree squirrels. One day I came out of the house with my fishing poles. You know what she did?"

The boys shook their heads. Vance's forehead wrinkled as he thought.

"Well, that dog, she looked at me for a bit, then disappeared. And I found her behind the barn digging worms!"

"Aw, no dog is that smart," Vance said.

Lexie laughed, patted his brother indulgently on the shoulder, and shaking his head said, "Vance, he's putting you on." Then he raced toward the house.

Vance glanced at Cotter as if to say, "That wasn't fair," and then raced after Lexie. Barking excitedly, Rainy followed. By the time they reached the gate into the barn lot, Vance had overtaken Lexie.

"Think their pictures will be any good?" Pippa asked, laughing.

Cotter nodded. "Probably good enough to satisfy them. Lexie has a real knack with the camera."

"Yeah. Vance is more interested in just looking. He forgets he has the camera until what he wants to take has already happened."

"I enjoyed today," Cotter said. "Thanks for suggesting it. I know I got some super shots."

"I had fun too."

He was still holding her hand. Then he slipped his arm around her waist. Pippa started to put her arm around him, but got tangled up in his camera straps. They both laughed. He started to lean over to kiss her, but decided not to in front of the boys.

"There are so many things I can draw and photograph here," he said almost sadly. "I don't think I'll be able to do them all by the end of the year."

"Do you have to leave then?" Pippa began to realize how much she wanted him to stay.

"Well, not really. I'd just set that time period. I have to get my stuff ready for some spring shows, and the deadline on my book on prairie plants is getting closer."

"Can't you do that here? You brought all your equipment and supplies, didn't you?"

"Yes, I did. I guess I wanted you to ask me to stay. The loft apartment is light and roomy. I've begun painting a scene of the farmstead from that big window. It's quite striking with the fall colors, the buildings, and the animals. I'd like to do a winter scene also. Maybe even a spring scene."

"Why don't you?" Pippa looked at his face as they walked slowly toward the barnyard. After getting used to his clean-shaven face, she decided that maybe she liked it better without the beard. She could see the play of his lips as he talked and as he mused. She especially liked how the corners turned up slightly when he was pleased at something.

The corners turned up now as he returned her gaze. "Okay, I'll stay. I must get down to serious work, so I'll have more time to help you and the boys."

"C'mon, slowpokes!" Lexie yelled at them. "Let's develop these pictures."

"The boys helped me set up my enlarger in the apartment bathroom," Cotter explained. "Makes a pretty good darkroom. I promised I'd teach them how to develop and print. I guess now is a good time." He tightened his pressure on her waist in parting and cut across the barnyard. Rube, dozing in the warm sun, merely looked up when he passed by her. She watched him as he joined the boys waiting at the machinery barn and disappeared up the flight of stairs to his apartment above the front half of the building.

Still feeling the pressure of his arm around her waist, Pippa entered her kitchen. Scampering in before she shut the door, Freewill made a beeline for his dish. Seeing it was empty, he sat on his haunches by it, boring his eyes into hers until she took the hint and poured him some milk.

Then she called her parents. Since Cotter's arrival, and her decision to keep the boys at home after school, she hadn't seen much of them. While Cotter and the boys were working in his bathroom-turned-darkroom, she chatted for most of an hour with her parents. Her voice was full of life and the excitement of living as she shared the latest news and activities of her family.

She replaced the phone in its cradle and leaned back

contentedly in the rocking chair in her kitchen. Freewill jumped into her lap and, after washing his face thoroughly, curled up to sleep. His soft purr and the ticking of the clock were the only sounds in the house until the muted hum of the furnace fan under the house joined in to remind her that cold weather was already here.

Though many people disliked winter, she loved it. She loved the crisp freshness of the air. She loved the feel of coming into a warm house after being out in the cold. She loved the look and feel of the animals with their thick, rich winter coats. She loved the unobstructed view of her land after the trees dropped their leaves. But most of all, she loved the comparative leisure of winter on a farm. No disking, no planting, no harvesting, no vaccinating, dehorning, castrating, or culling of cattle. No rushing urgencies. Those things belonged to the growing season. Now that nature was at rest, she could slow down also, with spare time to relax, to read, to watch TV. And to be with Cotter.

She savored that last thought, knowing that he would be around at least until spring.

She passed her hand over Freewill's short, soft fur. In the winter she had the luxury of spending part of the time like a cat—curled up in a warm place. In the winter there was only a few odd jobs and of course, the daily feeding of the stock. But feeding the animals was fun. She enjoyed watching the piglets and sows dive into their mash and the cattle savor their daily portion of grain. It was always a pleasant task to spear another huge round bale of hay with her tractor and drive with it to the pasture, and then watch the cattle bury their noses into their fragrant food as they pulled out mouthfuls of hay.

The odd jobs she still must do were not as much fun, but necessary. Since there was usually no immediate urgency, she could attend to them as she felt like it. She began to list them, to prioritize them in her mind. She wanted to cut out some more weed trees—hedge, locust, and cedar—in the pasture to maintain the grasses. There were the tractors to winterize. She planned to clean out the back section of the machinery barn and throw out some old junk and rearrange things to make more room. She would get more gravel to fill some mud holes around the machinery barn. And continual repair to fences and buildings was needed.

She thought of the various small repair jobs—the light in Vance's room wouldn't work, the refrigerator was making unusual noises, the hog lot gate needed a new hinge. And, she'd almost forgotten, she'd have to repair the barn stall where Rube butted off some boards when she was shut in there while the sheriff was digging up Herb Smith. Ugh! She had quickly assessed the damage at the time, but because of all the excitement and more pressing obligations, she hadn't done anything about it. She should get to it first as she would need that stall soon when the sows began to farrow.

First thing Monday morning. That would be her priority. Thinking about it cast a shadow over her pleasant mood. She hated that type of work—repairing damage that shouldn't have happened. Why should she have to do extra work because of a neurotic goat? Then she softened as she realized that Rube was only trying to protect her people. Pippa admitted that four strange men digging in the old barn shed was cause for alarm in the goat's one-track brain. Oh, well. The hole shouldn't take long to repair.

Then her mind wandered to pleasant times before Doug's death when she and he worked together in the slower pace of winter. Her memories added to her contentment, her peace.

Lexie bounded in, waving in front of her face a five-by-seven black-and-white photograph. "Mom, Mom! Look. I got a picture of a quail and I developed it!"

"Me too," Vance said, pushing another print into her hands.

Behind the boys came Cotter, smiling and nodding.

"I'm going to be a photographer when I grow up," Lexie announced. "I'll just play baseball as a hobby."

Pippa smiled at him. "That's a good idea, sweetie. Let me see your picture. Yours too, Vance." She took the two photographs and studied them. Lexie's was the better of the two, though she didn't say so. His flying quail was in focus. Vance had caught three birds in his picture, and though they were recognizable as quail, none of them were in good focus.

"These are fine, guys. Let's put them up on the wall." She stood up to tape them to the kitchen wall where other of the boys' pictures and writings were posted.

"Not yet," Lexie said, grabbing it back from her. "I want to take it to school."

Pippa turned to Vance. "You can put mine up," he said. "I'm going to take these feathers I found." He dug out of his pocket a fistful of tiny quail feathers to show her.

"Good. Maybe you'd like to read up some on quail to tell the class something about them also?"

"Yeah," Vance said, running into the living room to the bookcase to get out the bird book.

"How did your pictures turn out?" Pippa asked Cotter.

"I haven't developed them yet. We just did the two rolls the boys took."

"You shouldn't spend so much of your time with them. I know you're behind on your own work."

"I enjoy it." He grinned. "Part of my rent." As he left he said, "I'll do the feeding tonight. Enjoy your evening with the boys." Giving her no opportunity to object, he was gone.

At first she felt guilty that he was doing her chores. Then she shrugged her shoulders and returned to her rocker, picked up Freewill, who had promptly taken it over when she got up to post Vance's picture, and sat back down.

Lexie started chatting about the darkroom experience. Every other word seemed to be, "Cotter did this" or "Cotter said this."

Vance returned with the bird book and sat at the table. "Mom," he said seriously, "Cotter said that he was going to stay all winter."

"Yes, that's what he told me too." She looked at his face which was screwed in thought. "Is that okay with you?"

"Yeah!" Lexie said. "He said he'd teach me all about cameras and the darkroom. Maybe I could fix up a darkroom of my own. Cotter said the basement would be a good place, 'cause there's water there and only the two little windows we could cover to make it dark.'' His eyes were shining in eagerness.

"Sounds like a good idea, Lexie. What about you, Vance?" Pippa asked. "Is it all right if Cotter stays?"

"Well, I like him okay. I know he's helping you a lot. And he sure figured out how to get along with Rube. She doesn't hate him now, but she doesn't exactly trust him yet."

"Is that the way you feel too?"

"No." He paused, his eyebrows drawn in thought. "Well, maybe. We haven't known him long. He's not from around here, and we really don't know much about him."

"We know he had a great-great-something aunt that's buried out in front of our house," Lexie said. "That makes us almost neighbors."

"It doesn't either," Vance said.

Pippa studied her serious son. "What's bothering you about Cotter, Vance?"

"Well . . . " He hesitated.

"He doesn't like Cotter holding his arm around you," Lexie said, serious for once and looking at his brother.

Vance reddened and gave his brother a warning look and a shove.

"Is that it, Vance?" Pippa asked gently.

"Maybe." He looked at Pippa with tears in his eyes. "He isn't Daddy." Vance then began to cry.

Pippa cradled him in her arms, drew him back to her chair, and rocked him as she used to do when he was smaller. Vance was sobbing in her arms. Tears were welling up in Lexie's eyes too at the mention of his father. Pippa beckoned Lexie to her, put one arm around him, and drew him to the side of her chair. The boys were too big for both of them to be in her lap at once.

Since the boys rarely mentioned their father, she didn't know that they thought about him and missed him as much as she did. Until lately she hadn't been able to talk to them about him without breaking down herself. In their communications it was as if he never existed. Since they rarely referred to him, she thought the loss didn't affect them as it did her.

As she remembered how avidly they listened to the story of him and Rube, she realized she'd been wrong. She resolved then that she would talk about him.

"No, Vance, he isn't Daddy. No one will ever be him. He was a very special person, and we must remember everything about him always."

"I can remember when he and Rainy used to hunt," Lexie said. "He said Vance and I were too little to go with him. But he used his gun, not a camera."

"Yes, he was a good hunter and conservationist. He took only a few quail each year to keep the population down so the others would survive the winter. He loved animals as you do, Vance. He loved this farm, but most of all he loved *us*—you guys and me."

In spite of the boys' tears, Pippa's eyes were dry. She was talking about Doug to his sons calmly, without grief for losing him, without—she realized for the first time—without blaming him for leaving her with total responsibility.

Lexie managed to squeeze into the seat beside Pippa. Holding both boys, she rocked for a few minutes in silence.

"I remember when we were little he used to rock

us like this and sing 'A Froggie went a-wooing go,' "
Vance said, wiping the tears from his face with the
back of his sleeve.

"Yes. Would you like me to sing it to you?"

"No," Vance said, "that's Daddy's song."

"And you can't sing anyway," Lexie said, a mischievous grin breaking through his tears.

"No, I can't. Not like he could. You have his voice,
Lexie."

"What do I have?" Vance wiped the last moisture
off his face with the back of his hand.

"You have his caring nature—his love of the land
and his love of animals."

Vance smiled.

"Daddy is everywhere all around us, guys. Just
look." She swept her arm out to encompass the kitchen
as well as the view of the farm from the kitchen window. "And he is in each of you. When you miss him,
just look for him in yourselves and in each other."

"And in Rainy and Rube and the cattle?" Vance
asked.

"And Freewill?" Lexie had to mention his favorite.
The cat was walking around the three in the rocker,
checking to see if there was room for him too. Deciding
that there was, he jumped up on Lexie's shoulder and
curled his tail around the boy's neck.

"Yes, Freewill too. We have many happy memories
about Daddy. Think about them when you miss him.
And talk about him whenever you want to. His loving
spirit is always with us, helping us."

The boys seemed satisfied. As Pippa rocked slowly
in silence, they each savored the pieces of their father
that they remembered.

"Vance," she asked, "is it okay with you if Cotter stays around for a while? Because if it isn't, he can leave."

He didn't answer, but nodded his head. She looked at Lexie, who nodded more vigorously than Vance.

"And if he puts his arm around me sometimes?"

Vance turned his teary eyes to hers and lowered his eyebrows in thought as he studied her. "Yeah, it's okay," he said. Again Lexie nodded his approval.

"Good. Now let's get some supper."

Lexie jumped up first, upsetting Freewill's perch on his shoulder. "I'll fix it."

"I'll help," Vance said, joining his brother at the refrigerator. They were instantly in animated conversation about what to prepare.

Pippa leaned back with fatigue—not from the tramping over the pasture all afternoon so much as the emotional strain of the last few minutes. Yet she felt unburdened and light enough to float out of the chair. Cotter was doing her nightly feeding; the boys were fixing supper. But most important of all, her sons had just given her permission to love someone besides their father.

Chapter Ten

Monday morning was a good time to begin the long-delayed odd jobs, check them off the list. Since the weather had turned cold and wet, Pippa started first on the inside jobs. She armed herself with the toolbox and some boards to repair the wall in the barn stall that Rube damaged.

She had plenty of company. Rainy followed her and dashed into the dry, warm barn as soon as she opened the stall door. Once out of the weather, he immediately shook himself, spraying a fine moisture over Pippa's denim jacket and jeans.

Rube, drops of water clinging to her heavy coat, trotted behind Pippa and almost succeeded in following her into the stall. Pippa's first impulse was to let her in, but she knew two wet animals with her would be too crowded—and unpleasant. She wrinkled her nose when she got a whiff of Rube's wet wool. Besides, unlike Rainy who was content to lie in a corner and watch, the nosy goat wouldn't lie still. She would poke her nose in the hole, knock over Pippa's tools, or gently butt her, demanding attention. She was definitely in the way. Instead, Pippa opened the gate to the adjoining shed for her.

Out of the cold drizzle, Rube first investigated the calf trough to glean any feed left there. Not much luck. The calves had licked it clean. However, she found some ground corn spilled on the ground. She nosed around a bit, but soon decided the few grains mixed in with the straw and manure were not too appetizing. She stationed herself by the hole in the wall Pippa was patching where she could watch the proceedings. As Pippa surveyed the damage, she looked through the hole straight into the goat's never-veering stare. Unnerving!

Freewill was already in the barn when the others arrived. When Pippa first opened the stall door, she saw him playing with some brownish rope or cord on the floor by the hole. But when Rainy bounded in, the cat extricated himself from the cord, jumped onto the feed box, and then leaped higher to one of the cross beams above the manger. He crouched down. Except for the tip of his tail which twitched rhythmically, his body was motionless. His yellow eyes flicked from Pippa to the rafters where he searched for a mouse. He soon gave up his vigil. Too much noise and confusion for mice to be out. Any mouse worth the name would hide up in the loft in the small square bales of alfalfa. His eyes, like Rainy's and Rube's, watched Pippa's every motion.

Kneeling to be level with the hole and using the claws of her hammer, Pippa jerked out the battered and splintered pieces of board paneling and tossed them beside her on the barn floor. When the hole was squared up neatly between two studs, she took the measurements of the gap. So she could work more comfortably to nail in the new boards, she gathered up an armful of the old boards to take outside.

When she returned for the rest, she noticed the thin cord that Freewill had been playing with. It was all tangled around some disklike object. She kicked it aside before she recognized it as some sort of electronic tape. Curious, she picked it up carefully so as not to tangle it further or break it. It was an old five-inch reel-to-reel tape. A few feet of the tape had been unwound from the reel, but the rest seemed to be in fair condition. There was no writing on the reel to identify what it was.

She glanced up at Freewill as if to ask him where he found it. His inscrutable gaze gave no clue. On a hunch, she stuck her head into the hole in the partition where Rube broke through and looked down between the two thicknesses of wall. Inside the barn stall a protective paneling had been nailed around to about waist high to keep animals from hurting themselves on the sharp edges of the wooden studs. Behind that, nailed to the other edge of the upright two-by-eight studs that framed the barn, was the original clapboard siding of the old barn. The shed had been added many years after the barn was built, using that side of the barn for its western wall.

Between the two walls was a eight-inch, open, well-like space, plenty big enough for Freewill to climb into. Pippa peered down into the dark pit. She couldn't see anything, and not relishing the idea of sticking her hand into the space, ran to the house for a flashlight.

Down in the space, the light picked out a small, square cardboard box lying open.

She fished it out. It was the box for the reel of tape. Partly gnawed by mice, it was coated with grime and cobwebs. If there had been any labeling on the box, it was gone. Except for the box, all she found in the wall were mouse droppings, stale hayseeds, and old wasp nests. Wiping the cobwebs and dust off her hand on her jeans leg, she surmised that Freewill had crawled into the hole that Rube made. He must have batted at the box, somehow got tangled up in the tape, and dragged it out.

How would a tape get into the barn wall? And who would want to put it there? Crazy! She tried to think how long ago tapes like this were used. She knew cassettes were common in the 1960s. Before that, people used reel-to-reel machines, though not too many people owned them. But she had no idea when they had come into general use. The box and the tape were no help, except to tell her they were old. Twenty years ago? Thirty? Maybe even forty. She didn't know.

The tape couldn't have been put there when the barn was built in the 1860s—no way. There were certainly no electronic tapes then. She wondered when the paneling in the stall was done. It looked old—probably soon after the barn was built. Of course, someone could have taken off one of the paneling boards and dropped the tape in. Most probably someone, say about 1950 or afterward, hid it in the barn for some reason, and it accidently fell into the wall. Yes, that was more logical.

She studied the wall. She couldn't remember if there were any opening between the two studs. Rube had pounded it so much that she couldn't tell if that section had been tampered with earlier.

She circled the stall to see if there were any breaks in the paneling large enough to slip the tape box into. She found places where animals, probably horses, had chewed on the wood. There were marks where hooves had struck the protective wood paneling and a few loose knotholes. No breaks. But the sheriff's men were all over the shed, not just opposite the hole. Rube could have attacked the wall any place on the shed side of the stall. So, she reasoned, since she was able to burst through at this particular spot and not any other, it must have been weakened.

Someone surely put the tape there on purpose.

But why? Not a likely place to store a tape. But a good place to hide one.

She peered through the hole again. Rube was still staring at her from the shed. The goat's eyes seem to indicate that she knew the answer to the riddle, if she could only speak. Pippa laughed. Smart as the goat was, she couldn't know what happened years and years ago.

Directly behind Rube was the spot where the sheriff's men had dug out Herb Smith's body. Though the floor of the shed was now smoothed over and new straw laid, and the calves feeding in there night and morning had obliterated all evidence of the recent excavation, Pippa pictured it as it was a couple of weeks ago from Rube's viewpoint while penned in the stall watching the men uncover the skeleton. Did Rube know the men were exposing a man's body? Pippa had heard tales that some dogs could scent dead bodies that had been in the ground for years. Could goats? Nah!

Rube had just been upset with all the strange men and unusual activity.

Rube gave a low, pitiful, "Baa-a-a." Rainy joined her with a sharp bark. Freewill was silent as always, though his tail swished more rapidly.

Pippa studied the tape again. Could it have some connection to the body? There was the coincidence of proximity. Once again she became excited to think that she, and Rube and Freewill, might have discovered another clue to that murder. Just when she, the boys, and Cotter had all agreed that they could never find out how or why Herb and Ivy were killed, here came to light this tape not ten feet from where Herb's body was hastily buried.

But this was merely a coincidence—nothing more. No way could these two discoveries be connected, for the simple fact that there weren't any reel-to-reel tapes in 1876. For sure! Still, it was interesting.

She carefully gathered up the tape and its reel, dusted off the box, and took them to the kitchen table for safekeeping until she had time later to investigate further. Then she returned and quickly patched the hole. By this time all three animals had lost interest. Rainy was asleep. Rube was lying asleep in the deepest corner of the shed, her head turned back in her customary pose with her nose almost touching a back hoof protruding from her mass of curly wool. Freewill leaped up through the open trap door to the loft. There was a scurrying sound, followed by a feeble squeak as the tabby bagged another mouse.

All day Pippa worked on various odd jobs. The drizzle stopped about noon, allowing her to work outside. Since today wasn't one that Cotter was to help,

Pippa hadn't seen him. She thought about him, picturing his endearing grin and pleasant camaraderie.

She often glanced toward the machinery barn, but didn't see him. His van was still there, so he hadn't left. He was probably in his apartment painting or working in his darkroom. She wondered what he would do after winter was over. She didn't like to think about spring when he would leave. He had entered her life, become pals with the twins, and generally turned her philosophy of day-to-day survival to one of optimism and hope. All within three weeks!

With the boys chatting endlessly to him and from his own observation, he knew almost all there was to know about the Greenlees, but she knew very little about him. Had he ever been married? He was raised on a farm in east Texas, he said, but mentioned nothing else about his family except the ancestor Ivy Lewis and a living aunt in Denison whom he visited on his recent trip back after his things. He seemed not to need money—not wanting pay for his work—yet Pippa knew that the sale of art and photographs didn't usually bring in much income. Yet he wore nice clothes, had the best photography equipment, and an expensive van.

He wasn't secretive; he just didn't talk about himself, and she didn't ask. Perhaps she would now. She wanted to know all about him. Thinking of him kept a smile on her face as she worked.

When she saw the boys get off the bus, she waved at them, and finished putting the screws in the new hinge on the gate to the hog lot. Vance quickly changed into his work clothes and soon joined her to help with the evening feeding. He was full of how successful his report on quails was with the class, and how everyone envied him and Lexie for their professional cameras. Mr. Cunningham put Lexie's photograph on the board and asked Vance to bring his tomorrow.

"I'm glad this report turned out well. Happier results than the bone, eh?" Pippa asked, winking at him.

"Yeah. Only with Lexie's picture and my feathers, Mr. Cunningham thought at first that we were hunting out of season."

"Oh. I didn't think of that. The season isn't open yet," Pippa said. "What did you do?"

"Well, Lexie kept talking about shooting the quail— you know, shooting a picture. Mr. Cunningham and the kids thought he meant with a gun."

"But you put him straight?" Pippa was worried. She didn't want the conservation agent coming out to investigate.

"Sure. We showed our cameras and told how we took the pictures." Vance paused. "I really don't want to take my picture tomorrow 'cause it's not as good as Lexie's. Do you suppose Cotter will let me take one of his—a really good one?"

"Why, I don't know. We're almost finished here; why don't you go ask him?"

Vance ran off so gleefully toward Cotter's apartment that Pippa suspected that permission to visit Cotter was what Vance was after all the time. She had made it very clear to both boys that they were not to bother Cotter—to get permission every time they visited him.

When she entered the kitchen, expecting to see Lexie either doing his homework or preparing dinner—a job he would rather do than help with the chores—she saw him seated at the table engrossed in untangling the tape Freewill found in the old barn.

"Where'd this come from?" he asked, hardly looking up or even saying hello.

Pippa told him about finding it. "Can you untangle it so we can play it to see what it is?" she asked.

"I think so. There's only one break in it. I've already spliced that. It's kinda dirty, but I blew most of the dust off. I'm afraid to wipe it or I might ruin what's on it."

Lexie wound the loose tape back onto the reel. "Looks like it's all here." He studied the crumpled end. "Maybe a little at the beginning is ruined." Once again Lexie was showing his curiosity. Vance would have dismissed the tape as junk. Not Lexie. He repaired it to find out what it was. "What's on it, Mom?"

"I've no idea. Looks pretty beat up to me. And I don't know how long a sound will hold." Pippa didn't say anything about her wondering if there was any connection to Herb and Ivy. "We need a reel-to-reel tape recorder to find out, or to see if it's still any good."

"Yeah," Lexie said, disappointed. "All we got is cassette players." Then he jumped up, excited. "Hey, up in the drawer with all that family stuff—you know, that I was looking though Saturday? I saw an old tape player. It's in the box it came in, all wrapped up in newspapers." He was already halfway up the stairs. "I'll get it."

Pippa heard him thumping around upstairs, dropping books on the floor out of the drawer, and then bounding down the stairs carrying a bundle about the size of a small attaché case wrapped in stiff, yellowed newspaper and tied with strips of torn rags. He set it proudly on the table.

"How did you know it was a tape player?" Pippa asked. It looked like an ordinary box to her.

"I thought it might be another diary, so I looked. When I saw it was just an old machine, I wrapped it up again and put it back." He started ripping off the paper.

"Hold on, Lexie. Let's not tear the paper. Maybe there'll be something interesting we'd want to read. It's obviously an old paper."

Pippa carefully removed the newspaper, dated August 12, 1953, and smoothed it out for later reading. The box revealed a Bell & Howell tape recorder and player, seemingly in good condition.

"Gosh, it's an old model." Lexie said, crinkling his nose in disdain.

"Machines don't have to be the latest thing on the market to be good," Pippa said. "Let's see if it works." She plugged it in. Lexie pushed the play key and the spindle turned. The empty take-up reel turned smoothly.

"Yeah! It still works." After his first disapproval of such an old machine, Lexie was intrigued with it.

They positioned the full reel on its spindle. Together they studied the unfamiliar controls and consulted the manual, which was enclosed in the box, to be sure they knew how to operate it. They didn't want to take any chances of erasing the tape or damaging it in any way.

"Wish we had a blank tape to test it first," Pippa said. She had never used a reel-to-reel tape player. Lexie was impatient with her caution, wanting to push levers to see what they would do. After studying the manual and pressing each key in turn until she was satisfied that she knew how to operate it, she let Lexie position the tape reel. Following the arrows on the diagram, and with Pippa watching carefully every move, he wound the end of the tape around the knobs and recording device and onto the take-up reel.

When it was all ready, they looked at each other. Lexie crossed his fingers and squinted his eyes as he pressed the play key.

There were staticlike noises, screeches, and then a garbled voice from the crumpled tape at the beginning. The tape made a couple of turns before they could recognize the words, which were spoken in an old man's feeble voice. Pippa turned up the volume and adjusted the tone controls until they could understand what he was saying.

" . . . *the tenth, nineteen hundred and fifty-three. My grandniece give me this machine to talk into. She wants me to tell about things that used to be, back when I was a young'un and such. Well, I may get around to that. Don't know, though, 'cause I don't feel too good. I'm ninety-three years old and don't reckon I've got too many more days. Her asking about my boyhood days got me to thinking about some things. So before I die, I figure this is a good way for me to tell something I done when just a boy. Something I never told before. I reckon I've got enough yet in me to tell it. I'd thought about writing it down, but didn't think I was up to it.*

"*I'll not let no one see this here tape, or know nothing about it. Already figured out a place to hide it out in the barn. Not likely no one will find it until the barn's tore down, and by then I'll be gone. Okay. Now I'll check to see if this here machine is recording.*

My niece showed me how, but I might have forgot. I forget lots of stuff that's happened lately. But not my boyhood. Not what I'm about to tell now. Never.''

There was a few seconds' space in the tape with only background noises. Pippa and Lexie looked at each other in amazement. Lexie's eyes were big and full of wonder. Pippa clenched her hands so tightly that her fingernails made deep indentations in her palms.

''You suppose it's about . . . ?'' Lexie started to ask, cocking his head toward Ivy's grave.

''Shh,'' Pippa said, and held up her hand for him to wait. The old man's voice came back on stronger than before.

''The fool machine seems to be working all right. Now, first, I reckon I should do this right, like affidavits, so in case somebody does find this, they will know who I am.

I am Seth Greenlee. I've lived all my life on the Greenlee farm, first with my father Isaac Greenlee and after his death as partners with my brother Olin and his wife Opal. When Olin died, back in, '35, I stayed on with Olin's grandson, young Olin, but I didn't do no more farming after that, though I still owned half of the original farm. Young Olin bought a lot of adjoining land. I'm leaving my share in the farm to him.

''Now then, that tells who I am. I've got the family history all written down if whoever hears this is interested.

''Now what I want to tell into this machine is what happened starting on May 16, 1876, right here on the

*Katy tracks across from the barn, just where the tracks
pull away from the county road.''*

Pippa stopped the machine.

"Aw, Mom!" Lexie said. "Why'd you stop it?"
He was sitting on the edge of his chair squirming in
his eagerness to hear.

Just as thrilled as her son, Pippa said, "Because,
Lexie, I think here is the answer to how and why Ivy
Lewis and Herb Smith got murdered." She was doing
some arithmetic on a pad. "Take his age of ninety-
three years from 1953 when he made this tape. That
makes Seth about fifteen or sixteen years old at the
time of the murders!"

"Yeah, and according to Opal's diary, he was the
only one home then. C'mon, Mom, let's hear the rest!"

"No. We must wait until both Vance and Cotter can
listen with us." She was shaking in excitement so much
as she stood up that she had to hang on to the table
for a moment. "They should hear it along with us."
She looked at the clock on the wall—five-thirty. She
could wait. "Now, sweetie, you run and tell Cotter
that we would like him to come over about seven."
When Lexie frowned at the long wait, she added,
"Don't tell him about the tape or why we want him
to come. Don't tell Vance either. Let's get everything
done so we can listen without interruption."

Being in on a secret partly compensated Lexie for
not hearing the rest of the tape. "Okay," he conceded,
starting out the door.

"Remember, don't say anything, and come right
back."

Chapter Eleven

Though pressed by both Cotter and Vance, Lexie
hadn't told them anything, though he made it obvious
there was a big secret he knew and they didn't. Lexie
was so enjoying his role of knowing something Vance
didn't that he couldn't help taunting his brother with
his I-know-something-you-don't-know mannerisms
and expressions. Several times Pippa warned Lexie to
cut it out and cautioned Vance to be patient until time
for Cotter to come.

"Where'd that old tape player come from? What's
that tape on it? How come you won't tell me anything?" Vance kept asking his mother. The only answer he got was, "Just wait, sweetie. You'll find out
pretty soon."

Since finagling didn't get anything from Lexie
either, Vance countered his brother's advantage by one
of his own. He held up for them to see, but wouldn't
let them touch, an eight-by-ten photograph of Cotter's
that he could take to school.

"Wow!" Lexie said, his face lighted in admiration.

He envied Vance, wishing that he had been with Cotter to get such a picture. Too much stuff was happening all at the same time. Since Cotter arrived Lexie was having trouble knowing where to be to catch the action.

Vance's strategy worked. Beaming and with a superior shrug at Lexie for his dumb secret, he now took center stage.

"Beautiful," Pippa said, only that word couldn't possibly describe the scene. At the bottom of the photo in the left foreground was a clump of wild grasses. But the first thing that captured her eye, just above the tallest, ripening, grass seed head, was a brown-speckled quail in flight. The white markings around its head were plainly visible—even the bird's round brown eye. In the background the blue sky was sprinkled with white clouds spaced just right to draw the eye back to the quail. The leafless pecan tree and the bank of timber behind it were in line with the flying bird, obviously its destination.

It was more than an accurate nature photograph. It told a story of the bird startled from its secure home, and probably young ones, looking toward some distant refuge in the trees. Yet the sharpness of the focus on the grass in the foreground indicated that its pull was greater, in spite of some disturbance there that caused the flight. The slight blur in the distant trees showed the uncertainty of their protection. She recognized more beauty and meaning in this frozen scene than she had experienced when she was actually there. With his camera, Cotter had captured the essence of the moment for everyone to experience and understand.

"It's just beautiful," Pippa said again, at loss for anything else to say.

"Cool." Lexie couldn't take his eyes from it. When he reached out to take it, Vance held it back and shook his head.

"Cotter said I could take it to school," Vance said proudly. "And look—he's put his label on the back."

Cotter knocked lightly on the kitchen door and then came in. "What's all the secrecy about?" he asked, glancing curiously at the old tape-playing machine sitting by Pippa on the table. Then he noticed that they were admiring his photograph.

Before anyone could answer his question, Lexie asked him, "Do you think I'll ever be able to take a picture like this?"

Cotter was pleased that Pippa and the boys appreciated it. "If you work hard enough at it, learn all you can, and practice."

"Can I have a label like that to put on my pictures?" Lexie asked.

"Sure," Pippa answered. "I can make you some on the computer. You just write down what you want put on the label and I'll print it out. You too, Vance."

Cotter leaned over to Pippa. He touched his photograph, his finger landing on the quail. "After Vance brings it home, I want you to have it, Pippa."

Pippa was doubly delighted, both because Cotter wanted her to have it and because the photograph seemed to have some special meaning for her, but she didn't have time right then to think more about it.

The marvel of Cotter's photograph still didn't answer his question, which he immediately repeated. "Now, tell me, what's the big secret?"

Lexie had kept quiet as long as he could. Assuming what he thought was a good detective stance, he said,

"We've got an eyewitness account to the murders." With this incredible piece of information, he sat down at the table, anxious to hear the rest of the tape.

Before Cotter or Vance could object to Lexie's fantasy, Pippa explained, "No, this isn't more of Lexie's imagination. He's right."

She then described how she found the tape and played some of it on the old Bell & Howell brand player. She turned to her sons who were squirming in anticipation. "Now, guys, you sit still and listen." She indicated the chairs around the table. She sat down by the tape player, pulled out the chair next to her for Cotter, and continued speaking to the boys. "Don't interrupt. We'll talk about it later."

She held up two old pictures that Lexie found in the dresser drawer. "*Seth Greenlee as a young man in 1885,*" she read from the note on the back of the first. "*Seth in 1950, age ninety,*" she identified the second. Without his shaky handwriting that identified the pictures, none of them would have recognized the two as being the same person. Pippa glanced at Cotter, wondering what he'd look like at ninety-three.

Propping the pictures against the tape player where they could all see them, and spreading out on the table before her the Greenlee family tree chart, she started the tape from the beginning so Cotter and Vance could hear the part that she and Lexie had already listened to. At the spot she and Lexie had reached earlier, she stopped.

"Vance, do you know what this means?" she asked.

"Yeah! Old great-uncle Seth knows something about Ivy Lewis. He put it on this tape and then he hid the tape in the old barn wall.'' His eyes were filled with wonder. ''And Rube found it.''

''No, Freewill did,'' Lexie said.

''Well—'' Pippa laughed. ''Actually I did, but I wouldn't have without both Rube's and Freewill's help.''

Cotter was impatient. ''Let's hear the rest.''

Pippa rewound to repeat the beginning of Seth Greenlee's story.

''Now what I want to tell into this machine is what happened starting on May 16, 1876, right here on the Katy tracks across from the barn, just where the tracks pull away from the county road.

''A couple of days before that, on Sunday, Pa and Olin and Opal (my brother and his wife) caught the morning train at Ellis to Jeff City and left me to tend to the farm. That was the first time I'd ever been alone in my life. Though only sixteen at the time, I felt quite the man to handle everything by myself. The corn was in the ground, and it was too early yet to cut the wheat, so all I had to do was the chores and a bit of garden work. Being it was a slack time in the work was how come Pa asked Olin and Opal to go with him. This was his last term in the legislature, and he wanted 'em to know about lawmaking and such. He hoped Olin would follow him in politics someday.

''Anyway, I was home by myself and doing great shakes. Nary a bit of trouble. So on that afternoon, it was a Wednesday I remember, I got my dog, Red, and Pa's double-barreled shotgun and went hunting. I thought I'd surprise the folks with rabbit stew when they got home. See, Pa got a new Remmington-

*Whittmore double-barreled shotgun back a spell, and
I was raring to use it by myself. I put two of Pa's hand-
loaded shells into the breech all ready. Now Pa was
pretty particular about his shells, so I didn't take but
one extra one that I stuck in my pocket.*

*"Red and me, we hunted all over our land. We had
a hard time finding any rabbits 'cause it'd been a hard
winter and they was pretty scarce. Directly Red jumped
one, but I missed it. I forgot to cock it and when I did,
the rabbit was too far away. Excited, you know, and
I wasn't no whiz with the gun nohow. We had only the
one gun and Pa or Olin always used it.*

*"I've often thought about missing that rabbit. If I'd
hit it, I'd have gone on home and none of this would
have happened.*

"That's the twelve-gauge shotgun!" Lexie said.
"The one that killed the guy in the barn."

"Probably, but be quiet, Lexie," Pippa said. Cotter
grabbed her hand and held it in both of his. His hands
were clammy.

*"Well, it was getting nigh on to chore time, but I
crossed the tracks and hunted for a spell on Hargrove's
land. I didn't have no luck there neither, so I cut across
his field back home. Just when I got to the bend in the
tracks, where they head off from the road, I heard a
man shouting some words I couldn't catch. And there
was a woman screaming back, not scared, but mad.*

*"I knew right off there was some trouble. I didn't
want no part of it. I didn't recognize the voices, so I
grabbed ol' Red and sort of hunkered down in the grass
and brush on the other side of the little bank from*

them. Right there the railroad bed is cut down into the rise in the land. So there is a little bank running along the north side of the tracks. Anybody on the tracks can't see you if you're on that side of the bank.

"Well, them two, they was right on the railroad tracks and was fussing something awful. 'You take your filthy hands off me,' the woman says. She was a young thing, maybe a couple years older'n me. Probably seventeen or eighteen. Pretty too, with snappy eyes and black hair piled high on her head under a little hat. Real fancy.

" 'I'll do what I please with you,' the fella says, only he put in some cusswords. Now, he was dressed in a black suit and tie—fancy, like a city fella with lots of money and never done a day's work in his life. He looked like what my niece today would call a sissy. About my size, and I was five-nine. 'I'll do what I . . .' I won't say the cusswords he used. Some of 'em I never heard before. 'I'll do what I blankety-blank please with you. You're my woman.'

"She lit off up the tracks again and he run after her—running funny, sort of favoring his right leg—and jerked her about. She hit him with her bag right across his face and kicked his shin. 'You're nothing but a thieving outlaw,' she says. 'And Smith isn't your real name. My family was right. I can't imagine why I believed you inherited all that money you carry around.' They was scuffling around, her hitting him and him trying to grab her. 'Bank robber!' she says. 'I won't go on with you. I'll tell everybody who and what you are.'

"At that, he was madder'n a nest of riled yellow jackets. He sure wasn't the pantywaist that I first took

*him to be. His eyes was. . . . Well, I ain't never seen
the devil, but them eyes was mean enough for the devil.
And he was quick too. I figured he'd been in plenty
fights the way he dodged and spun. He caught his game
leg on the rail and stumbled, but was on his feet again
quick as a cat.*

*"Well, they struggled there right on the south shoul-
der of the tracks. It didn't take the fella long before
he knocked the lady down. Her bag flew out of her
hand over in the brush. Her hat come off and her hair
spilled out over the gravel. Still she kept on calling
him names, like coward, villain, outlaw, jailbird. She
should have known better 'cause it just made him even
madder. He started slapping her across the face. She
put her hands up to protect herself, kicking him, and
squirming and rolling back and forth down there in
the gravel against the rail.*

*"Sure, she was a plucky one. She didn't scream,
but just tried to protect herself. When he give her a
punch in the stomach, so hard that she couldn't get
her breath, I couldn't stand it no more. I had a gun
and a good hunting dog that I'd seen hang on to a
young coyote till he shook it dead. So I clumb over the
bank and down to the tracks with my gun pointed at
him, only I was so excited I again forgot to cock it. I
came on just like them pictures I seen in dime novels.
I was yelling, 'Let go that lady!'*

*"The fella, he stopped, real surprised, but not
scared. He glared at me like I was some country hick—
I guess I was, at that. He let go of the woman and
raised up, but he moved so fast I didn't even see him.
He grabbed the barrel of my gun, and with one motion,
whacked me across the stomach with the butt end and*

then swung it at Red, catching him in the air. Ol' Red jumped him the minute the fella come for me. He give Red a wallop on the head that stunned him. Plum grounded him with his head laying across one of the tracks. Not killed, though, just stunned.

"When the woman got up and started to back off— she didn't say nothing, but he musta heard her—he spun around and shot her. Without a word, he didn't even take time to look through the gun sights—I didn't see him cock the gun—but he pulled the trigger with the gun about on a level with his waist. Like they do nowadays in them movie westerns with a pistol, but this was my pa's long, heavy double-barreled shotgun. The feller sure knowed how to use a gun. He pulled the trigger and with almost the same movement put down the hammer on the other barrel ready to shoot again."

There was a long pause in the tape. Pippa's hand was almost hurting in Cotter's grip, though she said nothing. The boys were on the edges of their seats waiting for Seth to continue. Lexie mouthed a silent, "Wow!"

"And, oh, that poor girl. Blasted not more'n four foot away with a load of shot! Hit her in the chest. I'll never forget the expression on her face before it went blank. The blast knocked her backward. She fell and rolled down the shoulder off the cleared right-of-way into the brush, stopping face up. Her brown suit and tan blouse sort of blended with the undergrowth. You had to look hard to see her there.

"At first I was so scared that I just stood there dumb

and stared. Then I started to run to her. The fella whirled around toward me, the gun again at his waist level, ready to fire. I knowed my last shell was in the breech. He steadied the long gun with his left hand on the barrel. His right hand held it poised on his hip, his finger on the trigger. Red revived about that time. He growled and went for the man's left arm, causing the fella to swing the gun skyward.

"I jumped in under the raised gun to grab it. With Red's firm hold on the fella's wrist—I seen blood coming out—I didn't have no trouble pushing the gun barrel even further up away from me. If he pulled the trigger that last shell would go off harmlessly in the air. I reckon that's what I was hoping for.

"With Red hanging on from one side and me at him from the front, we soon knocked him down. Red lost his hold on his wrist. The fella was fighting both me and Red, and doing a good job of it. He knowed how to fight. I didn't. If Red wasn't there helping me, I'd have lost for sure.

"We was struggling over the gun. Me dodging his boots that were flying all around me. That was the first time I never seen a man fight with his feet. On the ground on his back, he flopped back and forth, trying to get away from Red. He held the gun in front of him parallel with his body, the muzzle near his head. He kept trying to point it out so he could shoot either Red or me, but the gun was too long and cumbersome to use like a pistol, which I reckoned he was used to using.

"Red was all over him, but couldn't get to his throat 'cause the fella used the gun barrel as a barrier. With the muzzle about even with the top of his head, the

fella moved it quicker'n I could see it from side to side. Red couldn't get to his neck, so he grabbed his right wrist.

"The fella let out a yell and let go of the gun with that hand. I seen my chance and seized its butt. I figured that with him holding it with just one hand, I could pull it away from him. But he was stronger'n I thought. When I yanked the butt of the gun outward, he was still holding on. I slipped both hands farther up the stock to get more leverage to pull it away. I clenched my right hand tighter for a stronger hold. My finger touched the trigger.

"The explosion close to my ear deafened me for a moment. The recoil knocked me back and made me drop the gun. I tripped over the rail and tumbled off the right-of-way. Red's ears took the same blast. He let go the man's wrist, whimpered, and run off shaking his head like his ears hurt him bad. Reckon they did, 'cause mine sure did.

"After all the commotion of yelling, cursing, barking, fighting, and the blast from the shotgun, it was mighty quiet. Not a sound 'cept the awful ringing in my ears. In the growing darkness, I lay sprawled in the tall grass close to the lady. I was afraid to move.

"Directly, Red crept back, whining and nosing me all over. I patted his head. My arm wasn't broke. I moved the rest of me and discovered that I was not shot or hurt. 'You okay?' I asked Red. He started licking my face and hopping around me in joy. Yes, he was fine.

"Since Red was standing by me—not guarding the fella, I knowed that at least for the time being, I wasn't in no danger. I reached out my hand to the lady. Dead.

I knowed, but I wanted to make sure. I got up, careful. I couldn't hardly stand, I was shaking so much. Trembling in every joint and muscle in my body. Reaction, I guess from the fight, because there was nothing wrong with me but a few bruises and torn pants where I slid over the ground.

"When I quit shaking, I looked at the outlaw. I can call him that now. That's what the lady called him, and his skill with the gun and fighting, not to mention the evil look in his eyes, sure pegged him an outlaw.

"Anyway, Red and I found him sprawled on his back between the rails. His arms was thrown out, his legs crooked—sort of folded under him as he fell. His face! He didn't have much left. After almost eighty years, I still can't think about it. I ain't never said nothing about it out loud till now. I'd helped with butchering hogs and cattle lots of time. But I never in my life seen a dead person. And here was two of 'em. And I killed 'em both. Well, no, not the lady directly, but my gun done it. It was my fault. And I pulled the trigger on the fella. The fact that he was an outlaw didn't help none. I sometimes still have nightmares about that fella. Like he's haunting me.

There was another long pause in the tape. Pippa was thinking that young Seth was only a few years older than her boys. What a terrible thing to happen. With tears in her eyes she looked at Cotter. He was shaking his head sadly. Seth's voice on the tape continued.

"I threw up. I don't know how long I would have stayed there if I didn't think about a freight train coming along. I had to do something.

"*I grabbed the fella's boots and pulled him off the tracks and into the brush alongside. Then I sat down panting from the exertion. No one from a speeding train could spot him here.*

"*What should I do? First I had enough sense to get my gun and take out both of the fired shells which I stuck in my pocket. But what about the dead bodies? I was in a predicament. Go for the law? That was the best thing to do. The honorable way. After all my father was representative from this district in the state capital. And I'd be a hero to my friends for standing up to an outlaw.*

"*But two dead people? I figured I'd be put on trial for murder, and probably sent to the pen for life. I couldn't prove that I didn't kill the lady. And I did kill the man. Self-defense? I'd have to prove it, and who would believe me? He was unarmed, and he was killed by my gun. Even though I knowed he was an outlaw, he didn't look like one. I myself didn't think so till he got mad and showed his true self. He fooled the young woman who surely liked him once. I figured she must have run away with him and somehow just found out what he really was. Maybe that's why she got off the train at Ellis—to get away from him. But it didn't work. He followed her.*

"*If I went to the law, even if they believed my story, I could see the disappointment and hurt in Pa's eyes that a Greenlee would do such a thing. And Opal. What would she think of me after that? I could take almost anything other than losing my family.*

"*Then if I told the sheriff, everybody would know. There'd be an investigation. Probably find out and publicize who the fella was. His outlaw gang would*

*then come looking for me. Maybe even the girl's family
would be gunning for me too. I'd never be safe. I'd
have to go far away. Leave the farm and the folks. I
couldn't do that neither.*

*"No, I'd have to take care of this by myself. Tell
nobody. Get rid of the bodies and nobody would ever
know.*

*"I felt better. It wouldn't be too hard to do. I never
seen the fella or the woman before. Not from this
county. They were dressed far too fine for any home
folks, even in town. Best get rid of 'em. But where? I
studied on all the places that I could bury them, but
each place had some problem. Better not bury 'em
together neither. Less likely anybody would find 'em
and connect me to 'em. I wanted some place that no
one would ever find. Couldn't be too far away neither.
The fella was too heavy.*

*"I finally lit on the shed of the barn. The more I
studied on it the better it seemed. I could dig there
without anybody who might pass by the road seeing
me. I could cover it with straw and feed the hogs in
there for a while to pack the ground back tight. Yeah.
The perfect place.*

*"I fetched the old wheelbarrow, and tugging and
dragging, got the outlaw in it. I thought I ought to get
rid of him first. It was dark by this time, so even if
anybody come along the road, they wouldn't see me.
But no one came. I wheeled him to the shed. I lit the
lantern and with pick and shovel started digging. I
even put the dirt I dug out on an old tarp so there
wouldn't be so much area messed up.*

*"It was hard work. Regular graves were six feet
deep, but I didn't go that deep. I figured eighteen inches*

or two feet would be enough. It was past midnight before I got the hole big enough. I dumped the fella out of the wheelbarrow into the hole. He landed on his side, sort of curled up, but I didn't touch him again. I shoveled the dirt back in quick. I tamped it down and pounded on it as I put it in so it wouldn't have to settle so much later and leave a sign somebody had dug there. I left a little mound over it for settling, because I could cover the whole shed floor with a thick layer of straw. Nobody would notice.

"And it worked out that way. Nobody never noticed or suspected a thing. For a couple of years later I volunteered to clean out the shed whenever it needed it. The first time I did it there was a sort of depression there where the grave was, but I filled it up with fresh dirt. After that the stock penned in there took care of it.

"Oh, I forgot to say. Though I couldn't hardly stand to touch him, I did look in his pockets—thought I might find out something about him. He had the usual stuff a fella carries, pocketknife, comb, handkerchief, matches, cigars, and wallet. Funny thing, though, there wasn't nothing to tell who he was. I figured outlaws was safer without identification, being on wanted posters and such.

"He also had a big wad of money. I didn't count it, but the outside bill was one hundred dollars, and the wad was big around as my shovel handle. I didn't touch it 'cause it was tainted money, probably from poor ladies like that black-headed one he just killed or from some bank robbery. Back then there was lots of talk about banks and trains being robbed in our part of Missouri.

"I burned the money and anything else he had on him that would burn. It was more money than I'd ever seen or ever would see again, but I wanted no part of it. My crime was bad enough without the sin of gaining from it.

"I was too tired to do anything about the dead lady, so I went to bed. I'd do it in the morning. Nobody would notice her body. Even if somebody walked up the tracks, they'd have to hunt for her to find her.

"Daylight come mighty quick, even though I didn't sleep a wink. I kept going over and over what happened. Could I have done anything different? Why did I think I needed to hunt across the tracks anyway? I kept seeing the lady's blank eyes staring but seeing nothing. And the outlaw fella's face. . . . I cried most of the night.

"I had to tend to the feeding before I could do anything about the lady. The stock was mighty hungry 'cause I didn't get around to feeding 'em the night before. Just as I was trying to decide what to do with her body, the folks come home. I wasn't expecting 'em till the next day, but Pa's committee work finished up early. They come in on the morning train and walked home from Ellis since I didn't know to fetch 'em in the buggy.

"Olin and Opal was mighty excited about the trip. Olin decided he would run for Pa's seat at the next election. Opal, she run up to me right off and hugged me, saying how proud she was of me taking care of things so good. I couldn't hardly stand it, knowing what I done and that poor girl still lying out there by the tracks. I loved Opal more'n any woman I'd known, besides Ma, of course. My sisters were older'n Olin

and I couldn't remember them being home much. But Opal, I knowed her all my life. When she married Olin and moved in, she sort of took over Ma's place. Mothering me, you know.

"I forced myself to tolerate Pa and Olin's congratulations at how well the stock was as long as I could. 'Anything happen while we were gone?' Opal asked. Since nothing ever happened, she really didn't expect to hear nothing, but I had to come up with some answer.

"I couldn't lie to her. So I says something else instead. I says, 'Red and me went hunting, but we didn't get no rabbit.' I told Pa that I shot but missed. I mentioned that there were three shells shot. So, I didn't lie. I didn't tell him that one of them shells— the one I didn't shoot—killed a woman, and the other one killed an outlaw. He thought I shot them other shells on rabbits too. He'd probably notice the gun had been shot, though I cleaned it as near like he always did as I could. He'd sure notice the empty shells cases. Anyways, I told him to take care of that in case he wondered.

"Olin teased me, 'You're sure no crack shot. You ought to practice more.'

" 'Yes,' Opal says, patting me on the shoulder, 'and what if some desperado of the Jesse James gang comes by robbing the train and finds you alone at home. You need to know how to protect yourself.'

"Olin says, 'I'll have to give you some lessons.' You know, Olin never did give me no lessons, 'cause I wouldn't touch a gun again. Ever.

"I couldn't stand no more. I run out to the barn like

I just thought of some job I had to do right then. Halfway to the barn, I jerked to a stop, remembering. I couldn't go there. There would never be any haven for me.''

Chapter Twelve

The end of the tape flapped as the takeup reel continued to turn. Pippa pressed the STOP key. The only sound in the room was the ceaseless ticking of the clock. Abruptly brought back to the present, she, as well as Cotter and the boys, needed time to absorb what they had just heard.

"He's not finished," Pippa almost whispered. "Surely there's more on the other side." She switched the reels and threaded the tape from the full reel around the posts to the empty reel, ready to play.

"Do you boys understand what we've just heard?" Cotter asked.

"Yeah," Vance said. "That's Ivy for sure in the unknown grave, and she was shot by the guy I found in the barn. Herb Smith, the guy she ran off with."

"Right. Did you catch that Seth even heard her call him Smith?" Everyone nodded.

"Our great-uncle, Seth, accidentally killed this Smith guy because he was trying to save your great-aunt.'' The wonder of it quieted Lexie as nothing else had done. ''We are related after all, Cotter.''

''Let's just say we are connected,'' Cotter said. He gave Pippa a quick look to catch her reaction.

''I like Seth. He sounds nice,'' Vance said, then asked Pippa, ''Did Daddy know him?''

Pippa consulted the family genealogy chart. ''No. Seth died before Daddy was born, in 1954. That was just a few months after he made this tape.''

''Listening to him is just like he's still alive,'' Lexie said. ''Cool.''

''And Herb *was* truly an outlaw, just like our sheriff said he was. He killed Ivy in cold blood,'' Vance said. He grinned selfconsciously at his use of words—more like Lexie would say.

''Shh,'' Pippa said as sputters of sound came from the second side of the tape. Cotter scooted his chair closer to Pippa.

The old man's voice continued, even more feeble than before. Pippa turned up the volume. Cotter reached for her hand again. Pippa put her other hand over it as they listened.

''I don't know if I can keep on. Ought to rest a spell, but I best finish this now or I might not get back to it. Don't want the folks here to know nothing about it. Since I've been so poorly, they don't much leave me alone, so I best keep on while they're all gone to town. My hand's shaking so I can hardly hold this little ol' microphone up to my mouth to talk in. Shucks, I used to be able to toss around hundred-pound sacks of feed like they was nothing more'n loaves of Opal's bread. Now, I can't hold up this microphone for more'n fifteen

minutes without I get all shaky. Maybe if I support it on the chair arm, the machine will still pick up my voice.

"Now, where was I? Oh, yeah. The folks come home and made over me for taking care of the place so well, and me feeling so guilty that I was sick. If they only knowed what I'd been up to while they was gone! I couldn't tell them. Opal looked at me sort of funny like she knowed something was bothering me, but she didn't say nothing. Neither then nor in the weeks later when I took spells of staying to myself, which I never used to do.

"After the woman's body was discovered, I think Opal suspected that I must have seen something. She never asked me. Many times I wanted to tell her, but couldn't bear to see the disappointment and loathing she would feel toward me. Now I wish I had. She wouldn't have hated me, I know now. It wasn't in her to hate anyone, especially not me. Mighta helped me too. But she's gone and I can't do nothing about it now.

"Now back to my story. I had the outlaw hid good enough. When Pa happened to pass by the barn shed, all he said was how proud he was of me to clean it out. I could see he was pleased I'd done a chore I hated without him even asking. But what about the lady? Poor thing laying out there dead. I couldn't do nothing about her. I had to leave her all alone out there in the weather with bugs and varmints.

"Pa and Olin were home all day and the next and next, never giving me a chance to even go out to the tracks and cover her up. Opal was watching me close, 'cause I was acting kinda puny. I couldn't eat. I'd *break out in sweat one minute and shake the next. She finally made me lie down on the divan and covered me with a quilt. Never let me out of her sight, fussing over me all the time, talking about how lucky it was they come home early before I took sick.*

"I told her it was high time she and Olin had some babies so she wouldn't mother me all the time. She laughed and agreed that would be nice. But that didn't stop her from fussing over me and me getting sicker all the time. Not sick like she thought, though.

"The killing was on a Wednesday. The folks come home on Thursday morning, and it wasn't till Saturday that the woman's body was found. How it happened was like this. Saturday morning when me and Pa and Olin went out to feed, some of the hogs were missing. Pa told me to go across the tracks to look for 'em. Opal, seeing how distraught I was, said she'd go because I wasn't well enough to be traipsing around after hogs all day.

"Well, Pa, he wouldn't hear to that. With three men on the place he wouldn't let Opal do a man's work. Pa was funny that way. Men had their work and women had theirs. So he give in to Opal's objection to me going—we always give in to Opal—and he grumbled that he'd go hisself. I finished the chores and looked for any job I could do to occupy myself. Nothing helped. All I could do was fret and stew. Maybe he wouldn't find her. I didn't know whether I wished he would or wished that he wouldn't. Either way was bad. Maybe the coyotes or dogs drug her off. Or—a horrible thought come to me. What if our runaway hogs found her? I got sick again.

"Pa was gone a long time, two hours or more.

Finally he hollered and give his shrill whistle that we could hear all over the farm. Pa whistled again two or three times. The sound come from where the lady's body was by the tracks. Olin was in the field, but he heard it and come running. So did Opal, who come flying out the house.

"*Opal and Olin run to him, for they suspected something was amiss. I went, but kinda slow-like. I knowed exactly what was wrong, but Olin and Opal didn't, of course. Pa was standing there, staring down at the dead woman, supporting hisself on his thick walking stick like he'd fall over without it. Olin put his arm around Opal and pulled her away. But she got a good look first. I couldn't take my eyes off the body. No animal had bothered her. It wasn't hot in May, so the body wasn't in too bad shape. Pretty much like I last seen her, only deader.*

"*Do you know her?*", *I managed to say. Pa knowed 'most everybody in the whole congressional district. If she did come from around here, he'd know her.*

" '*No,*' *he said. His voice didn't sound like Pa. Sorta feeble and trembly. 'Must a-fallen off the train. Or been pushed,' he said, seeing the black bruises on her face.*

"*Then he seen the blood on her chest that was dried brownish and at first glance looked like dirt—not bright red as it was when I seen her. It didn't show up right off against her brownish suit. 'Lord save us all,' Pa prayed. 'She's been shot.'*

"*He started to order me home when he seen how upset I was, but changed his mind and sent me to the depot in Ellis to wire the sheriff.*

"*I run the mile down the tracks to Ellis without even*

slowing down. I busted into the depot and shook awake George Worley—he was the agent at that time. It was a spell before I got my breath enough to blurt out, 'George, send a wire to the sheriff. There's a dead woman on the tracks up by our place.'

"If I was ever the center of attention, I was then. There were several fellas around the building loafing and passing the time. Also Maude, George's wife. They plied me with questions faster'n I could answer them. But directly I told 'em the body was a young fancy-dressed woman we didn't know. And by the looks of her she'd been there two or three days. I didn't let on just exactly how long she'd been there, but of course I knowed.

"George wired the sheriff right off. Then everybody started talking about who she could be and recalling a woman like that getting off the train. 'Specially Maude. She remembered it the best. She said that a young, pretty, and well-dressed woman got off the train on Wednesday evening. She thought it was Wednesday. The others figured back and after some arguing back and forth, agreed that was the day. They all of 'em noticed her. Maude said the woman was mad when she got off. Then just before the train started up again, a dark-suited young man jumped off.'Musta twisted his ankle,' Maude said, ' 'cause he limped.' The girl and he argued for a spell, then she took off up the tracks after the train, him following.

" 'That's the same girl,' Maude kept saying. 'That's who the dead girl is.' She swelled up important-like. She loved to tell the gossip and now she had some real stuff to say—a killing. She went on saying that she suspected foul play by the way the man looked. He was

mean. She went on to say she thought about speaking to the girl and maybe helping her. 'Course, she didn't think none of that at all or she would have called the sheriff right then. She just liked to embroider on the truth to make it even better. My run down the tracks calmed me some, but I trembled like a fit caught me when I thought what all Maude would tell if she really knowed the truth. When Maude seen how peaked I looked, she come up to me to take care of me like Opal did. I pushed her off.

"Everybody wondered what happened to the fella with her. 'Of course,' they all agreed, 'he musta murdered her and run off. Likely one of the outlaws that are running free in the county.' Then they started discussing how dilatory our law was that there's so much violence still even with the war over for ten years.

"With most of Ellis following me, I run back to Pa who was still standing guard over the body. The sheriff and some railroad fella got there mighty quick—they come on one of them little hand carts the railroad men use to repair the tracks.

"The sheriff looked over the situation. Nobody recognized the woman. The people from Ellis told how she got off the eastbound train with a man. The sheriff seen that she was shot in the chest with a shotgun.

" 'Did the man carry a gun?' he asked. No, everybody agreed that he wasn't carrying nothing and the lady had only a small handbag, too small for a shotgun.

"Everybody there, me included, tramped around looking for the fella's body. I'd have done anything to get away from the sight of her. 'Course, we didn't find no body or nothing else, 'cept the woman's bag which

was almost hidden in some leaves about ten feet from her.

"In it there was only a few dollars, a change of clothes, some nightclothes, comb, and brush—woman stuff like that. Nothing to identify who she was or where she come from. Not even a stub from her train ticket.

"The railroad fellas and the sheriff, they agreed they had to do something with the body right away. It'd already been three days. Them days there wasn't no funeral parlors and embalming. Besides, the body was way past that by then. Pa sent me to the barn for picks and shovels—the same ones I used to bury the outlaw. I even had to knock some of the dirt off the shovel before I took it to them. All the men but the sheriff took turns digging the grave right beside where she lay.

"Maude went back to Ellis for some clean clothes to dress the body. Opal brought some stuff from our house to help her. They washed her face and hands and scrubbed off the caked and dried blood. They combed out her long hair till it flowed across her shoulders, only they didn't fix it up on her head like she wore it. Her hair was the only part of her that still looked pretty. They closed her eyes and one of the railroad fellas give Maude quarters to put one in each eye to keep them shut. After her eyes were closed, I could look at her without my stomach turning over. The women even put some rouge on her cheeks before they dressed her in the new clothes that covered her chest.

"When they got done with her, she looked much better. Not pretty like she was when I first seen her, all lively a-sassing the man, but neat and not so grue-

some. She still looked dead. I stared at her for a long time so I could fix that picture in my mind to get rid of the other horror.

"Olin and another neighbor, who had some already-cut lumber, hammered together a crude coffin. They laid the body in it carefully. All stretched out nice and proper, hands across her chest like they ought to be in a regular burial. Then when the fellas—I helped some—got the grave down to six feet, they lowered the coffin into it. Pa sent me to fetch his Bible, and he said a few words over her, and we all said the Lord's Prayer. George and Olin shoveled the dirt back in.

"While they was working, the sheriff talked to everybody, and took down lots of notes. He took her clothes and handbag and announced that there'd be an inquest. But he wasn't too interested in this strange lady, and I figured he wouldn't do much more investigating. And I was right. He didn't. Pa and some people from Ellis who seen the couple get off the train went to town the next day to the official inquest. The murder was written up in the weekly paper, but that was all. In a few weeks everybody forgot it. Except me.

"And some railroad workers.

"A few days after we buried her, I went by her grave and seen that somebody had spread on top of the mound a thick layer of white chat—like what's used on the bed of the train tracks. And there were some wild daisies sprinkled over the gravel.

"The railroad men never forgot. As the years went by, they tended the grave, keeping the weeds off. They even placed a border of smooth round rocks around the grave. Then a blank headstone and footstone showed up. Them fella had to go to a lot of trouble,

*for them stones didn't come from around here 'cause
there ain't no rocks in this country 'cept along the river
bluffs. Ever year around Decoration Day there was
flowers put on the grave. And still to this day the grave
is tended—much better'n most of the graveyards in the
county.*

*"Now I never done a thing to the grave. Never
touched it. Wanted to, many times. I was glad that she
wasn't forgot, though we never learned who she was.
Never."*

There was a long pause in the tape. Pippa was about
to turn it off, thinking that was the end, when Seth
continued.

*"That's the story that I had to get off my chest. It's
been haunting me all these years. I can't let young
Olin or his children find this tape. Maybe it can come
to light when everybody who ever knowed me is dead.
I've picked out the right place to hide it—between the
walls in the barn stall nearest the outlaw fella's body.
Just in case anybody finds the bones, and searches
around, then this record will explain how they got
there. Not a soul on earth but me knows where he lies.
And I don't know who he is.*

*"I've tried to live a good life. Always lived on this
farm. I farmed with my father, and with Olin and opal
and their children and grandchildren. I helped 'em all
I could to make up to 'em for me for not building my
own house. For you see, I never married. Couldn't
take the chance of staining any more lives or bringing
any children into the world to inherit my sin.*

"May God forgive me, for I can't forgive myself."

Though Pippa played the tape to the end, there was nothing more.

Old Seth had explained everything. The four people studied the photographs of the young and the old Seth, while the clock measured out the seconds, reminding them that time was slipping away, just as it had for Seth Greenlee. Pippa and Cotter were sad and glad at the same time. Sad for Seth's wasted life, and glad that they still had time for happiness.

Cotter squeezed Pippa's hand. Bathing in the warmth and understanding from his eyes, Pippa smiled at him through the tears Seth's story evoked. There by the tracks where she first saw Cotter, years ago two young lives were lost. Although Seth lived a long time, his life was ruined as surely as Ivy's. The third life didn't matter. In her mind the outlaw deserved what he got.

Eerie. Pippa knew that Cotter had similar thoughts—the sadness of past events that occurred here with their ancestors and the potentials of their own futures.

Lexie was the first to speak. "Cool," he said as he hugged Freewill. While the tape was playing, Freewill had taken turns sitting on Cotter's and Pippa's laps. Now, purring softly, he was cradled in Lexie's arms.

"Out of this world," Vance agreed.

Sobered by the tape, the boys were silent for a few minutes before starting their usual chatter.

"The ghosts can rest now that Uncle Seth has told us who they are and why they are buried here," Lexie said.

When Vance groaned and started to object, Pippa put her hand on the boy's arm to deter him. In a way Lexie was right. There were unsolved presences—call them ghosts, if you like. Or spirits. "Yes, sweetie, they can rest."

And her personal presence? Doug's spirit? He could rest too. She was all right now. She squeezed Cotter's hand.

"Do you know what I'm going to do?" Cotter said, rising. "I'm going to make a wooden marker for my great-aunt Ivy's grave. I've got just the board in my van. Want to help me?" His glance included both boys.

"Yeah!" They both jumped up, eager to be active again.

"But not for Herb," Vance said. "The sheriff took him away. He's gone and he was a bad man."

"Right," Cotter said. "Nothing for Herb."

"He ruined my great-uncle Seth's life," Vance said. "It was all his fault, not Uncle Seth's."

"I wish Seth could have believed that," Pippa said. "Then his life might have been happier."

"Yeah," Vance said. His freckled face screwed up in thought. "Don't you think that he knows now, Mommy? Now that we have found his tape and know it's not his fault?"

"Perhaps."

Vance paused in thought. "And Daddy? He knows too, doesn't he, that we miss him all the time, but Cotter is here with us and it's okay now?"

"Yes, Vance, sweetie, I'm sure he does." A warm, comforting wave crept over Pippa. She and Cotter exchanged quick glances.

"Go now, you guys"—her order included Cotter—"make that marker for Ivy, and I'll fix us some hot chocolate and cookies to celebrate."

Chapter Thirteen

The next afternoon, even though there was a cold, drizzling rain typical of early November, Pippa, Cotter, and Rainy were at Ivy's grave. Cotter had driven a pole into the ground at the head of the grave without disturbing the weathered stone placed there unknown years ago. While Pippa held the plaque straight about a foot from the ground, he drilled holes to screw it on the post.

Shivering from the wetness dripping off him, Rainy looked at Pippa with sorrowful eyes as if to ask why they were out in this weather.

The night before Cotter and the twins had sawed the board into the shape of a shield, sanded it smooth, and applied a coat of weatherproof varnish. Propping the wet board up to dry, they returned to Pippa's kitchen to plan the wording. Lexie wanted some dramatic writing such as, "Here lies a beautiful lady shot down without reason by a bloody villain." Vance and Pippa laughed at him, but Cotter was kinder. He said there wasn't room for so many words. Since Ivy Lewis was

171

Cotter's relative, the Greenlees agreed that he should be the one to decide what to say. Early in the morning Cotter had painted in the lettering.

After Cotter tightened down the last decorative screw, which matched the indented gold lettering edged in black, he stepped back to admire his handiwork and take a picture of the grave with the marker in place. Its simple artistry fit the lonely and wild location.

> *IVY LEWIS*
> *July 12, 1858–May 15, 1876*
> *We now know who you are*
> *Rest in peace*

Tears came to Pippa's eyes. "It's so sad. And wonderful. All these years without anyone knowing who she was. Her family hoping she'd come home. Yet, for some reason, her grave has never been forgotten. Most strangers found dead like her would have been buried and the site immediately forgotten and returned to the wild. But not her." She removed the anemic-looking plastic tulips and replaced them with a fresh wreath of cedar. Entwined in the fragrant greenery were vines of wine-colored buckbrush berries and orange-red bittersweet berries.

The click of Cotter's camera seemed only an echo to a soft, "Bob White," coming from up the tracks. From farther away another bird answered.

Kneeling beside her, Cotter put his left arm over her shoulder. The blue surface of her blazer was wet from the light rain. "This is a fitting end to a tragic romance," she said.

"Or the beginning of a beautiful one." Cotter ran the fingers of his right hand down her cheek to wipe off a tear. Since Cotter's comment was not a question, Pippa didn't reply. A surge of happiness such as she hadn't felt for many months replaced her sympathy for Ivy's tragedy. The two quail repeated their soft calls to find each other, this time closer together.

"I wrote a long letter to my aunt in Denison," Cotter said. "I'll send her a picture of the grave with the marker as soon as I get these developed." He patted his camera, now protected from the drizzle in its black case hanging over his shoulder.

Pippa thought that was thoughtful of him.

"I also wrote an article for the local paper giving the whole story of Ivy and this 'Herb Smith,' or whatever his real name was. The editor was excited about it. He's going to put a short account in today's paper on the front page. Then he's going to use my whole story in Sunday's paper."

"You're a writer too?" Pippa asked, greatly impressed.

"Yes. To get my pictures published, I often have to write the copy. I took the editor some of my pictures of the grave and the sheriff digging out the bones."

"You don't miss anything, do you?"

"Well, I try not to. My camera is always near me. I never know when I might see a good subject." He stepped back to photograph the grave with the new wreath. "Stand there by the marker. This will go with Sunday's story."

Just then the boys jumped off the school bus. Rainy barked his greeting as he loped toward them. Seeing their mother and Cotter at the grave, they dropped their backpacks by the mailbox and joined them.

"Shouldn't the boys be in the picture too?"

Cotter agreed. While explaining what they were doing, he took several shots.

"Rube ought to be here," Vance said. "She discovered Herb and great-uncle Seth's tape."

"And Freewill," Lexie said, racing back across the road to find the cat without seeing if Cotter agreed.

"Okay," Cotter said to Vance, "go get Rube."

Vance had no trouble finding Rube. Now that the rain had stopped and the sun was trying to peep from behind the dark clouds in the west, she was at the barnyard gate waiting for someone to notice her. Vance led her back, trotting beside her as he held on to one of her horns. Though she would have followed him, he kept a good grip on her. He still didn't trust her around Cotter.

Rube watched Cotter carefully as Vance positioned her by the marker where Cotter told him, but she showed no signs of hostility. When Cotter put his hands on her flank to push her closer to Vance, she obeyed readily.

Lexie couldn't find Freewill. The group at the grave heard him calling as he dashed through the house and out the back to the barn. He was almost in tears when he came back empty-handed.

"That's okay, Lexie," Cotter said. "When you find him, we'll come back out to take you both."

"You ought to be in the picture too," Lexie said. He took his camera out of its case. He had picked it up in his run through the house.

While Lexie was taking his photographs, Vance was

studying the grave site with its new marker. "You know, Mom, we ought to keep this ground around here mowed off."

"You're right. That old fence is of no use now and about fallen down. We can tear it out, and I could brush-hog this corner here." She looked at the V-shaped area that belonged to no one and had therefore been allowed to grow up. There were several tall cottonwood trees and a few smaller maples that could stay to shade the area.

"It'd be like a real cemetery, then, wouldn't it?"

"Yes, or a little park. Good idea, sweetie."

Anxious to see how his film turned out, Lexie dragged Cotter to his darkroom. After figuring out what they could do to improve the grave site, Pippa and Vance returned to the house.

"How was school today?" Pippa asked the routine question parents always ask, expecting a noncommittal, "Okay."

However, Vance's smile made his freckles dance across his eager face. "Great!" Shuffling through his school pack for his notebook, he brought out Cotter's photograph that he had carefully placed there to keep it protected. "When Mr. Cunningham asked me if I brought my picture to put up on the bulletin board beside Lexie's, I said mine wasn't good enough. So I showed him Cotter's."

He was squirming out of his jacket as he talked. "Mom, you should have seen his face. He liked it just like we did. Then he held it up in front of the class and used it to teach about wildlife." He pointed to the seed heads of the tall grass in the foreground. "Did you notice that you can even see some ripe seeds there just ready to fall out?''

When Pippa shook her head, he continued, ''I didn't either until Mr. Cunningham showed us. And he knew just exactly what kind of grass that is.'' Vance tapped his finger on the print. ''Bluestem. I remembered. It's some prairie grass that almost got extincted.'' He screwed up his face. ''I think that's what he said.''

''Extinct,'' Pippa said. ''That means gone forever.''

''Oh. Did you know we had that on our place?''

''Yes, sweetie, I did. We have lots of it in the pastures. It's spreading now that we know how to protect it.''

''So it won't be''—he paused to say the word—''extinct''?

''Right.''

''That's cool.''

''Sounds like you sure scored lots of points with your teacher today.''

''Yeah. But Mom, that wasn't all. I wish Lexie was here 'cause he'll want to help tell you. But he'll just blurt it all out in front of Cotter, so I better tell you before they come back.''

His serious manner startled Pippa. ''What about Cotter?'' This teacher, though an excellent one, was beginning to worry her after his reporting of Vance's bone. *Now* what had he done to upset her family? Or what had Cotter done?

Vance loved having his mother's undivided attention. ''Well, after Mr. Cunningham finished talking, he looked on the back of the picture at Cotter's label.'' He paused to let that piece of information sink in.

"What's so important about that?" she asked. "Most artists and photographers identify their work."

"Yeah, but Mom, when he saw Cotter's name, he flipped. He got real excited and started asking me all kinds of questions about Cotter. Did I know him? How come I had one of his pictures? I thought sure I'd done something wrong, or maybe Cotter had."

Pippa's uneasiness returned. Perhaps Cotter was too good to be true. Last night she didn't understand why he asked the boys not to say anything yet about solving the murder. That puzzled her. But today she thought that she knew why when he told her about his visit to the newspaper. He didn't want the boys to scoop his story. Sensible precaution. He wanted to prevent rumors and distorted facts so he could tell them right. Smart move. But was there more behind it than that?

"Mom, you're not listening," Vance complained. She had a bad habit of tuning the boys out when her mind went into another direction. His accusation brought her attention back to him.

"Huh? I'm sorry. What did you say?"

"I said that Mr. Cunningham asked me if he was *the* Cotter Lewis, the famous photographer. Lexie and I said that he was a photographer, but we didn't know about him being famous. Then Mr. Cunningham looked in his cabinet behind his desk where he keeps stuff and got out a big book of pictures. On the back was a picture of Cotter. Only he still had that beard."

"Really!" Cotter had a book published? She could hardly believe it.

"Yeah. And all the pictures in that book were Cotter's. It was called *In the Mood*. Isn't that a dumb name for a book of pictures?"

"No, not for Cotter's pictures, if they are like this one." She picked up Cotter's photo of the quail. "They do evoke a mood. What were the pictures about?"

"Nature stuff. Animals, trees, rivers, scenes. That kind of stuff. Lots of colored and black-and-white pictures that covered the whole page. And the book was a big one." He held out his hands to indicate a book about ten by twelve inches.

"Was there any writing besides the pictures?"

"Yeah, but I didn't get a chance to read it. Mr. Cunningham kept moving the book about. He never gave it to me. He asked if I thought Cotter would come in to talk to our class. I said I'd ask. Do you think he would?"

"I expect so. He seems to like kids."

As they were talking, she heard the sound of a familiar car slow down in front of her place, and then speed up. The newspaper delivery. She sent Vance out after the paper, anxious to see what it said. He ran back, pulling off the plastic bag and unrolling the newspaper. Across the top in heavy print was: *120-YEAR-OLD MURDER SOLVED*. Under the headline in smaller print they read: *Unknown Grave at Ellis Linked to Bones Recently Discovered.*

In the center of the front page was a great-looking picture of Cotter with the caption, "Prizewinning photojournalist and artist, Cotter Lewis of Denison, Texas, and the Greenlee family of Ellis discover the identities of both bodies killed on May 16, 1876."

"We're famous!" Vance shouted.

"Well, it seems that Cotter really is!" Pippa was stunned with what Vance said about his teacher, but more so by the article in the paper. And relieved. This was good news about Cotter. Not . . . She didn't finish that thought.

She devoured the article trying to see what else it said about Cotter, while trying to remember if she had ever before heard of his work. During the past two years her own little world had completely swamped her. She hadn't kept up with much else, not having the time or the inclination to read magazines or listen to public radio stations that featured artistic people.

The short article gave only brief details of Ivy and the outlaw, ending with an announcement that there would be a long feature with full details and Cotter Lewis's photographs in Sunday's paper.

After glancing at the headlines, Vance didn't want to read any farther without sharing it with his brother. He opened the kitchen door and yelled out for Lexie to come see what was in the paper about them. Lexie bounded in, leaving gates and doors open in his eagerness. A few minutes later when Cotter reached a place where he could stop with the darkroom work, he came over also.

"Wow!" was Lexie's word to express whatever emotion he felt. Cotter's renown didn't impress him as much as seeing his own name printed in the paper. He and Vance had their heads together reading again the brief mention of them in helping find the evidence that solved the mystery.

"Better'n making up stuff, huh?" Vance said to Lexie.

"Yeah. This is hot stuff." He looked at his mother. "I'm going to be a detective when I grow up."

"Why didn't you tell us you were famous?" Pippa

asked Cotter, half teasing and half hurt that he hadn't told her more about himself.

"I didn't think I was." He stroked his chin, worried that what the paper said about his reputation might make a difference to Pippa.

"It says here, prizewinning," Pippa said. "Doesn't that make you famous?"

"Well—" Cotter ran his hand through his unruly hair and grinned at her. He certainly didn't look like a celebrity in his jeans still damp and muddy from putting the marker on Ivy's grave and his sloppy sweatshirt reeking of hypo and fixer. "I've done all right with my work. Had a few one-man shows. Gotten a few awards."

"Our teacher showed us your book when we gave him your photograph of the quail," Vance said.

Cotter was pleased to know their teacher knew of him and had his book. "Did he like the picture?"

"And how!" Lexie said. "We spent all science period learning about quail and nature and stuff like that."

"All the stuff in your picture," Vance said, handing it back to him.

"And everything he talked about is right here on our farm," Lexie said. "He spent the whole period on just that one picture. Really cool!"

When the boys described more fully the impromptu lesson Mr. Cunningham had taught, Cotter seemed genuinely flattered at the attention given him. Of course, he would visit their class—they just had to let him know when.

Then he handed the photograph to Pippa. "I want your mother to have this, guys. She may see even more in the picture than your teacher did."

Vance puckered his forehead. "What?"

Cotter put out his hand toward Pippa to let her answer.

Just as clearly as the first time Pippa saw the picture, she sensed the mood the scene evoked. But this time the message was personal as if Cotter was saying something to her alone.

"What, Mommy?" Vance urged. "What do you see?"

Pippa paused to think how to put into words that the boys could understand just what the photograph meant to you. "I see that in spite of troubles at home, or even loss of someone very dear"—she pointed to the tall grass in the foreground of the photo—"in spite of the seeming safety of reaching an uncertain haven"—she touched the pecan tree—"that home is still the best place to be." She hugged the boys and reached out her hand to Cotter. "Because there you are not alone."

Vance seemed to understand. His serious face studied the picture and he nodded. Lexie cast a cursory glance at the photograph and said, "Still looks like our pasture and an ol' quail to me."

Later when Cotter and Pippa were alone doing the feeding, she asked, "How many books have you published?"

"Five of photographs and three of my paintings."

Surprised at the number, she paused as she was spreading out the grain in the calf trough.

"You never told us. You just said you went to arts fairs to sell your work."

"Well, that's a great part of what I do," he said, opening the gate to let the calves in. "I told you I was working on a book about prairie grasses." When Pippa nodded that he did, he took her hands, his eyes on hers, and asked, "Does it make any difference?"

"No, of course not. It's just that you know everything about us, but we don't know much about you."

"Then ask. I'm not one to go about talking about myself, but I'll tell you anything you want to know."

There was so much she wanted to know that she didn't know where to begin. About his family, his schooling—many questions. But this wasn't the place or time for long biographies. Instead she asked, "Was the reason you wanted to stay here to take photographs?"

"Yes, I told you that. At first that's what it was, to help my research on the prairie plants. But I saw right away, with the kids, the animals, and this great farm, that there was material here for other shows and books—certainly magazine articles—if I could interest my agent and publisher. Subjects such as the modern family farm or better yet, women farmers. And pesky farm animals," he added and laughed as Rube was standing directly behind him, eyeing his every move.

After a pause, he gazed long at Pippa. "But I'll admit that almost immediately and certainly after a couple of days, I knew I wanted to stay for a completely different reason that had nothing to do with my work."

"To solve the mystery of the grave?" she teased him.

"You know that isn't what I meant. Though, yes, that did enter into it."

"To scoop everyone in the press and perhaps write a Pulitzer Prize-winning story about Ivy, Seth, and Herb?" She couldn't stop baiting him like this.

"That's icing on the cake. It may get me a Pulitzer, but that's still not the reason."

Pippa was enjoying her role. She couldn't stop. "To get free room—"

Cotter put his arms around her and pulled her to him. His kiss stopped her in mid-sentence. Holding her tight and kissing her again, he said, "Yes, I wanted to stay just to get a free room over two tractors, a combine and drill, and no telling how many other machines." When she started to say something, he put his fingers on her mouth and shook his head. "And to shave off my trademark beard." He stroked his bare chin. "To muck out the hog lot, to save a dozen errant pigs and a damsel in distress from a diesel locomotive." When Pippa turned down her mouth and shook her head at his "damsel in distress," he paused, knowing he was on dangerous ground.

Rube was standing close beside him. He automatically reached out and petted her as he would have Rainy. "And play second fiddle to a goat," he continued. "That's why I want to stay here. Satisfied?"

He gave her a quick kiss and ran his fingers lightly over her cheek.

"Anything else?" Pippa continued her baiting as she kissed him back.

"Yes, now that you mention it, there is. I stayed so I could wade through mud every time I walk into the machinery barn to my apartment."

"I'll get a load of gravel."

"Good. In that case I might stay permanently. But getting inside without muddying my boots may not be reason enough. I'll need more company. Perhaps come spring, a move into the big nest in the tall prairie grass as Mr. Quail?''

Pippa raised her eyebrows in surprise. Did he mean what she thought? Her knees were so weak she would have crumpled if Cotter wasn't holding her up. When she didn't answer, he realized how vague his question was. Switching from his teasing manner, he restated his question, his tone and manner this time serious. ''What I mean is that we spend the winter getting to know each other better with the possibility of marriage at the end?''

He brushed aside one of the curls from her forehead so he could hold both her eyes with his. She didn't know how to answer him. Finding it easier to continue the light tone, she said, ''That might be arranged. Only you'll have to ask permission first.''

Rube was rubbing her head affectionately against his leg. ''Rube has just given hers,'' Cotter said. ''And Rainy and Freewill liked me even before you did.''

Pippa laughed.

''So I'm all set? I've got permission?'' he asked.

''No, I mean people permission,'' Pippa said, speaking seriously, not in the light, jesting tone she'd been using.

''Sure, I'll ask your parents.'' Cotter was serious, also.

''Not them either,'' Pippa said. ''I mean my sons.'' She cocked her head to indicate the back lawn where Vance and Lexie were playing roughhouse with Rainy. Freewill was watching the activity from a safe perch on one of the gate posts.

''Oh, yes. Good idea.'' Arm-in-arm they crossed

the barnyard to the gate. Rube kept step with them, by Cotter's side.

"You know," he said, stroking his chin, and grinning at Pippa, "I think I'll let my beard grow back."

Freewill jumped onto his shoulder as they opened the gate to join the boys and Rainy.